22/4/15

The Bourne Supremacy

ROBERT LUDLUM

Level 5

Retold by David Maule
Series Editors: Andy Hopkins and Jocelyn Potter

Pearson Education Limited
Edinburgh Gate, Harlow,
Essex CM20 2JE, England
and Associated Companies throughout the world.

ISBN: 978-1-4082-3170-8

This edition first published by Pearson Education Ltd 2011

3 5 7 9 10 8 6 4 2

Original copyright © Robert Ludlum 1986
This edition arranged with the Orion Publishing Group Ltd, London
Illustration by Chris King

Set in 11/14pt Bembo
Printed in China
SWTC/02

Published by Pearson Education Limited in association with
Penguin Books Ltd, and both companies being subsidiaries of Pearson PLC

For a complete list of the titles available in the Penguin Readers series please go to
www.penguinreaders.com. Alternatively, write to your local Pearson Longman office
or to: Penguin Readers Marketing Department, Pearson Education,
Edinburgh Gate, Harlow, Essex CM20 2JE, England.

Contents

Introduction

Webb screamed, falling onto the bed. Then he turned over and stared
at the ceiling as lost memories suddenly came back to him. He thought
of bodies falling under his gun or his knife. And now he knew the two
men within him. One was the man he wanted to be, but for now he
had to be the other.

David Webb teaches at a small college in Maine, in the United
States. His wife has just been kidnapped and now he understands
that he will have to become somebody else, somebody he was
earlier in his life—the highly-skilled assassin who was known
as Jason Bourne. Webb does not want to become Bourne again
but he has no choice.

In the 1970s, more than ten years before *The Bourne Supremacy*
begins, Webb was working in Cambodia for the Central
Intelligence Agency. In neighboring Vietnam, the war being
fought between the Americans and the North Vietnamese was
coming to an end. One day a plane from across the border
killed his first wife and their children. Crazy with anger, Webb
ran away to Saigon, where he was asked to join a top secret
special operations group known as Medusa. While working
for Medusa, behind enemy lines, Webb met the original Jason
Bourne. He killed him, because Bourne was working for the
North Vietnamese.

Years later, Webb used the name Jason Bourne in a secret
operation that went badly wrong. He was shot in the head and
lost his memory. However, his employers in the United States
thought he had gone out of control and had stolen a great deal
of government money. They—and his real enemies—tried to
kill him. The story of how Bourne, with the help of a young
Canadian woman called Marie, discovers who he is and defeats

the assassins, is told in the first of the three best-known Bourne books: *The Bourne Identity*. This is also a Penguin Reader.

In *The Bourne Supremacy*, the second book in the series, Bourne is married to Marie, but is forced away from his quiet, normal life in Maine to Hong Kong. This is 1985, and the colony is moving into its last few years under British control.

The island of Hong Kong became a British colony in 1842, after a war between Britain and China. In 1860, following China's defeat in a second war, Britain obtained a part of the mainland. However, most of the colony was gained when a 99-year agreement between the two countries was signed in 1898. In the years before this agreement was due to end, Britain realized that it could not keep the small part of Hong Kong that was given without limit of time. So, in the 1980s, there were discussions between the two countries for the whole of Hong Kong to return to China in 1997. There was an atmosphere of tension and uncertainty. Nobody was sure what the future might bring, and it is in this situation that most of the action of this novel takes place.

In the earlier part of the twentieth century there were great changes in China, leading to a Communist government and the start of the People's Republic of China in 1949 under the leadership of Mao Zedong. Those who opposed Communism were known as Nationalists; they kept control of the island of Taiwan, which today is called the Republic of China. However, as we shall see in the book, some people in the People's Republic remained opposed to the Communist system.

The Bourne Identity, *The Bourne Supremacy* and the third book, *The Bourne Ultimatum*, are all best-sellers and were made into movies starring Matt Damon. The stories in the films, however, are very different from the books. In the film of The Bourne Supremacy, Jason Bourne is living in Goa, India. Marie is killed very early in the story, and later the action moves to Europe and the United States.

Robert Ludlum was born in New York City in 1927 and grew up in New Jersey. His talents first led him in the direction of acting, and he appeared in a Broadway show at the age of sixteen. From 1945 to 1947 he served as a soldier in the South Pacific, and his first serious piece of writing was a 200-page description of his time there. However, after returning home and graduating from college, he continued with his acting career. In the 1950s, he worked as a stage and television actor. He then became a producer of plays for theaters in New York and other cities.

His first novel, *The Scarlatti Inheritance*, appeared in 1971 and became a bestseller. This was followed by *The Osterman Weekend*, which was later made into a movie. The hero of the book, John Tanner, works with the CIA to discover Soviet agents among his closest friends. This sets the style of Ludlum's heroes as strong, independent men who battle against organizations, sometimes secret ones. The action always takes place against a background of real-world events.

From the mid-1970s, Ludlum was a full-time writer. He wrote more than twenty novels. Over 200 million copies have been sold and the books have been translated into twenty-nine languages. Five of the novels have been filmed, and two more are in development.

Robert Ludlum died in Florida in 2001. However, since then a number of novels have appeared in his name, based on writing that was incomplete at the time of his death, and four more Bourne novels have been produced by the writer Eric Van Lustbader.

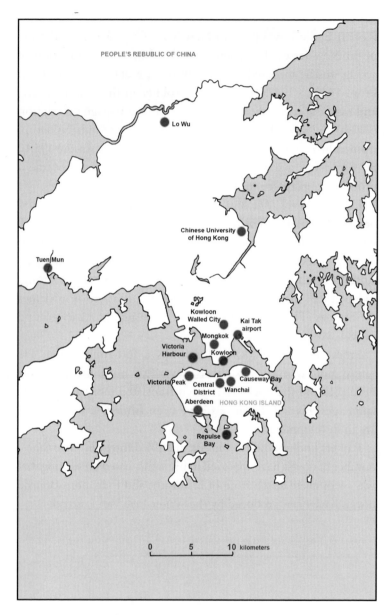

Hong Kong in the 1980s

Chapter 1   The Holy Man

Kowloon, 1985. Across the water from Hong Kong Island, the land belonged to Hong Kong, not to China, but here politics took second place to the more important business of filling stomachs.

As the sun went down, a small motorboat moved into an empty space on the west side of the harbor. The noisy crowds of locals and tourists were silenced as people noticed the figure climbing up the ladder. He was a holy man, tall and dressed from head to foot in pure white cloth, which hid most of his face. He walked slowly through the crowds and disappeared into the busy streets.

The priest went east on Salisbury Road until he reached the Peninsula Hotel, then turned north into Nathan Road, to the start of the brightly-lit Golden Mile. He walked for ten minutes, sometimes giving commands to the same short, strong Chinese man who sometimes followed him, sometimes ran ahead.

The priest nodded to him, twice, then turned and walked through the entrance to a nightclub. The Chinese man stayed outside, his hand inside his jacket, his eyes watching the street.

Inside the nightclub, moving colored lights cut through the heavy smoke. On the stage a rock group sang fast and loudly, the music changing between western and Chinese.

The priest stood for a moment looking across the large, crowded room. A fat, well-dressed man approached him.

"May I help you, Holy One?" asked the manager.

The priest leaned forward and whispered a name. The manager's eyes opened wider, then he bowed and showed the priest to a small table by the wall.

"Would you like something to drink, Holy One?" he asked.

"Goat's milk, if you have it. If not, plain water. Thank you."

The manager bowed and moved away. This priest had spoken

1

the name of a powerful taipan*, and on this particular evening the taipan was in the building. But it was not the job of the manager to tell him that the priest had arrived. The holy one had made that clear. When the taipan was ready, a man would come to him.

"Send a kitchen boy down the street for some goat's milk," said the manager to the head waiter. "Tell him to be quick."

The holy man sat quietly at the table; then suddenly, several tables away, a match was struck and quickly put out—then another, and finally a third. This last one was held under a long, black cigarette. The priest moved his head toward the flame and the poorly-dressed Chinese man smoking the cigarette. Their eyes met and the holy man nodded slowly.

Seconds later the smoker's table was in flames. Fire shot up from the surface, spreading quickly to the menus and food baskets. The smoker screamed and turned the table over. Waiters ran in and customers on all sides jumped from their chairs as the fire on the floor, for no obvious reason, spread around their feet. Then there was even greater trouble. Two waiters had come close to the poorly-dressed man. He attacked them with open hands and fast kicks. The manager, now shouting, moved in, then back again after a well-placed kick to his stomach. As three more waiters ran into the fight in defense of their boss, men and women began hitting each other. The rock group played louder and faster. The poorly-dressed man looked across the room at the table next to the wall. The chair was empty.

The priest had stepped through a door near the entrance to the nightclub. Down the passage a man stood up straight, his hand reaching inside his jacket for a heavy gun. The holy man moved slowly toward him.

"Everything is peaceful," he repeated quietly as he approached.

* taipan: a powerful businessman in Hong Kong or China

2

The guard was beside a door. He pointed the gun. "Are you lost, priest? What are you doing here?" he said.

The guard had no chance. The priest pulled out a long, sharp knife and cut the man's wrist, then swung the blade across his throat. The dead man fell to the floor.

The priest put the knife back into the cloth of his robe, then took out an Uzi machine gun. He kicked the door open and ran inside.

Five men, all taipans, were sitting around a table with pots of tea and alcoholic drinks near each. They looked up, their faces twisted in fear. A burst of bullets flew into them.

The killer knelt down by a pool of blood. He pulled out a square of dark cloth from his sleeve and laid it on the floor, then wrote a name on it in the blood. As he left the room, he removed the knife from his robe and pushed it into his belt. Then he opened the door and moved around the shouting, fighting crowd. Nothing had changed, but why should it? He had left only thirty seconds ago.

The killer priest pulled the robe from his body, dropped it and the Uzi on the floor next to the door, then took off a pair of thin gloves and put them into his pockets.

The priest and his assistant fought their way through the frightened crowd at the door and into the street. They moved through the onlookers and were joined by the short, strong man who had waited outside. He took the killer's arm and pulled him into a narrow street, then took two towels from his jacket. One was soft and dry; the other, in a plastic bag, was warm and wet.

The killer took the wet towel and began rubbing it over his face, removing the make-up that had made him look more Chinese. He dried himself with the second one, then straightened his tie. "Go," he said to the other two. They disappeared into the crowds. And a well-dressed Westerner walked out into the streets.

Inside the nightclub the trouble had suddenly stopped.

Waiters were calming down the customers and clearing up the mess. The manager looked around the room and saw the pile of white cloth in front of the door to the offices. White cloth, pure white—the priest? The *door*! The *taipan*! The *conference*! His face wet with fear, he ran between the tables and knelt down in front of the robe. He saw the machine gun sticking out and spots of blood on the cloth.

"What is it?" asked a second man in a suit, the manager's brother and assistant. "Oh *God*!" he swore under his breath as the manager picked up the gun in the white robe.

"Come!" ordered the manager, getting to his feet and moving toward the door. In the passage the dead guard lay in a river of his own blood. Inside the conference room the manager approached one of the five dead bodies. He wiped away the blood and stared at the face. "We are dead," he whispered. "Kowloon is dead. Hong Kong is dead. All are dead. This man is the Vice-Premier of the People's Republic of China."

"Here! *Look*!" The manager's brother picked up a piece of dark cloth from the floor and stared at the name in blood on it: *JASON BOURNE*.

The manager moved across and stared too. "Oh my God!" he said, his whole body shaking. "He's come back. The killer has come back to Asia! *Jason Bourne*! He's come *back*!"

Chapter 2 The Undersecretary

The sun fell behind the Sangre de Cristo Mountains in central Colorado as the Cobra helicopter landed a hundred meters from a large wooden house. The house was not on any public map and its messages were secret from enemies and also from friends. This was a place for work that was so sensitive that the planners could not be seen together.

The doors of the Cobra opened and a man climbed down.

McAllister walked to an open door at the side of the house, where a guard was waiting. The guard led him along the passage until they reached a door with a red light above it. The guard knocked. The light flashed and he opened the door.

"Your guest, sir," he said.

"Thank you *very* much," replied a voice. The surprised McAllister recognized it from many radio and television news broadcasts over the years.

A gray-haired, well-dressed man walked across the room, his hand held out. "Mr. Undersecretary, how good of you to come. My name is Raymond Havilland."

"I certainly know who you are, Mr. Ambassador."

"I'm not an ambassador any more, McAllister, but I still have plenty of work. Please take a seat." The two men sat down. "Mr. McAllister," Havilland said, "You are in a position to help your country greatly."

McAllister studied the ambassador's face. "In what way?"

"The Far East," said the diplomat. "You've served your government well for many years in Asia, and since you returned your judgments have been very valuable in helping us make decisions in that troubled part of the world."

"Thank you," said McAllister. "But how can I help you?"

Havilland stared at him for a moment, then lowered his voice.

"You must promise never to tell what you hear to anybody."

"I promise," said McAllister.

"Have you heard the name Jason Bourne?"

"Of course," answered McAllister. "Thirty-five to forty murders. He killed anybody if the price was right. They say he was an American. I don't know. He disappeared."

Havilland leaned forward. "Let me tell you the truth. The Jason Bourne you've just described never existed. He was an invention."

"You can't be serious."

"Never more so. Those were violent times in the Far East—drugs and money. Whenever an important killing took place, we made it known that Jason Bourne was responsible."

"But he was," said a confused McAllister. "There were the signs, *his* signs. Everybody knew it."

"Everybody *believed* it, Mr. Undersecretary. A telephone call to the police, a small piece of clothing sent in the mail ... They were all part of the plan."

"The plan? What are you talking about?"

"Jason Bourne—the original Jason Bourne—was working for the enemy and he died with a bullet in his head in a place called Tam Quan during the last months of the Vietnam war. Several years later the man who killed him used his name for one of our operations, an operation that nearly succeeded but went out of control. That man was shot. Part of his brain was blown away and the result was that he lost his memory. He didn't know who he was or who he was meant to be."

"Good *Lord* ..."

"A Canadian woman who became his friend and is now his wife helped him to discover who he was. She forced him to examine his words, his abilities, then to make contacts that would lead him back to us. But we didn't understand. We thought he was working for the other side, that he had killed three of our people and disappeared with a large amount of money—over five million dollars of government money. We tried to kill him."

"But what was the plan? What were you trying to do?" McAllister asked.

"To find and trap the most dangerous assassin in Europe."

"Carlos?"

"You're quick, Mr. Undersecretary."

"Who else was there? In Asia, people were always comparing

Bourne and Carlos."

"Those comparisons were encouraged by the planners, a group known as Treadstone Seventy-one. That's a name you should remember."

"So where is this man now?" said McAllister.

"His real name is David Webb. At the moment he's teaching at a small college in Maine. And we need him back in Asia."

"Have you spoken to him?"

"We can't approach him. He doesn't trust anything or anybody from Washington, and it's difficult to blame him for that."

"I'm beginning to understand," McAllister said. "You want me to speak to this David Webb and persuade him to return to Asia. For another operation—to kill again?"

"Yes," said McAllister.

"And you think because I know Asia well, he'll listen to me."

"Yes."

"May I know who you want him to kill?"

"You may. He's a Chinese minister of state, Sheng Chouyang."

"Sheng? I know him. But why would anybody in the West want him dead? He has Marxist views on a centralized state, but he respects the profits of Western economics."

The old diplomat spoke slowly, choosing his words carefully. "Sheng Chouyang is not the man you know. He's a secret Nationalist, with connections to Taiwan."

"Sheng ... a Nationalist? I don't believe you!"

"He and his people plan to govern Hong Kong. He's putting all of the colony's finance companies under the control of a group of bankers from both Hong Kong and China. The agreement with Britain ends in 1997, and this seems like a good form of preparation for Chinese control. But these bankers are all in Sheng's pay, so it will be *Sheng's* control, when he feels ready. It could be in a month, or two months. Or next week."

"It's crazy!" said McAllister.

"Of course it is," said Havilland. "It will never work. But then Beijing will blame American and Taiwanese money, working together with the British. The Chinese army will attack Kowloon, and the island, and the result could start a world war."

"My God," McAllister whispered. "It can't happen."

"No, it can't," said the diplomat. "We can't allow it to."

"But why *Webb* as the assassin? Why Jason Bourne?"

"Because they are saying in Kowloon that he's back in Asia, that he's killed again."

"*Webb*?"

"No, Bourne. The invention."

"How?"

"Sheng Chouyang has brought him back. A few nights ago the Vice-Premier of the People's Republic was murdered in Kowloon when no one in Beijing knew he was there."

"Why did Sheng want him dead?" asked McAllister.

"He opposed Sheng's plans. But now, if Webb can find and kill this Bourne impostor, and take his place, he can reach Sheng."

"But Webb won't do this."

"Then we must give him a strong reason to do so."

Chapter 3 David Webb

Exhausted from a hard run, David Webb reached the college gym. Mo Panov had told him that if there were times when terrible memories broke into his mind, the best way to handle them was with exercise.

Morris Panov was the only person besides Marie who could talk to him. They had worked together for months, as patient and doctor, and finally as friends.

Webb opened the door of the gym and walked down a white-walled passage until he reached the changing room. His clothes were in a closet at the far end. As he walked toward it, his eyes fixed on something. A folded note had been taped to its door. He pulled it off and opened it. It was from the gym manager and said, *Your wife called. She wants you to call as soon as you can. She says it's urgent. Ralph.*

Webb opened the closet and took some change from his pants pocket. He ran to a pay phone on the wall and rang Marie.

"David, come home," she said. "There's somebody here you must see. Quickly, darling."

♦

Edward McAllister introduced himself, letting Webb know that he had quite a high position in the State Department. "Mr. Webb," McAllister began, "I'm not your enemy. In fact, I want to help you, to protect you."

"What are you talking about?"

"Somebody got their hands on the Treadstone file."

"Who did?"

"A British Intelligence agent from Hong Kong, somebody the CIA has trusted for years. He flew into Washington and asked to be given all the information there was on Jason Bourne."

"He had to have a very good reason," Webb said.

"He did. Jason Bourne is back. He's killed again. In Kowloon."

Webb did not move. Instead he studied McAllister, as a man might watch a snake. "What the *hell* are you talking about? Jason Bourne—*that* Jason Bourne— doesn't exist any more. He never did."

"You know that and we know that, but in Asia his story is very much alive. You created it, Mr. Webb."

"This British Intelligence agent, the one who took the file—can we trust him?"

9

"It doesn't matter now. He's dead. He was shot two nights ago in Kowloon, in his office."

"But why?" Webb asked.

"We think that somebody wanted the Treadstone file—the file on Jason Bourne—and asked the British guy to get it. Then the Briton was killed, to break the connection."

"But *why*?" said Marie, her hand holding Webb's wrist.

"Because a woman was killed, the wife of a rich Hong Kong banker named Yao Ming. She had lovers, but he looked the other way—she was young and beautiful. She also used drugs. Her last lover was a drug dealer. He was killing his competitors, so he was marked for death."

"But he would have a dozen bodyguards."

"That's true, and that's why they needed the best assassin. Bourne."

"But there *is* no Bourne," Webb said, closing his eyes.

"Somebody is using his name," said McAllister, "and he's very good at his job. Two weeks ago the drug dealer and Yao Ming's wife were shot in their bed in the Hotel Lisboa in Macao."

"And this banker, Yao Ming," Webb said. "Had he worked with British Intelligence?"

"Yes," said McAllister. "His connections in Beijing made him very helpful. So he used this relationship to get the file on Jason Bourne, the assassin who killed his wife. Now he knows where you live, where you work."

Webb stared at the undersecretary for a few seconds. "It's a good story. Why don't I believe it, Mr. McAllister?"

"Probably because you can't trust your own government, and you have very little reason to do so. However, I'll make sure you're safe."

◆

Edward McAllister climbed into the passenger seat of his own State

Department car. "Let's get out of here," he said to the driver.

The car started forward. For several minutes neither man spoke. Finally the driver asked, "How did everything go?"

"The preparation is done," McAllister said.

"I'm glad to hear it."

"Are you? Then I'm glad, too." McAllister raised his shaking right hand and rubbed his forehead. "No, I'm not!" he said suddenly. "I can't believe what I've done."

♦

In his office at the college, David Webb hung up the phone. The line had been busy for nearly an hour, and there was no one his wife could talk with on the telephone for an hour, not even her father, her mother, or her two brothers in Canada. *Something was wrong.* Webb raced out of his small office.

Reaching his house, he brought the car to a sudden stop as he jumped out of the seat and ran up the path to his front door. He stopped, staring. The door was open.

Webb ran inside and searched the ground floor. Then he went upstairs, listening for any kind of sound. For these moments he knew and accepted the fact that he was the killer—the animal— that Jason Bourne had been. If his wife was above, he would kill whoever tried to harm her—or who had harmed her already.

Nothing. The two rooms were empty. His Marie was not there.

"Marie! *Marie!*" Then he saw it. A note lying on the pillow on her side of the bed: "*A wife for a wife, Jason Bourne. She is wounded but not dead, as mine is dead. You know where to find me, and her. Maybe we can do business; I have enemies, too.*"

Webb screamed, falling onto the bed. Then he turned over and stared at the ceiling as lost memories suddenly came back to him. He thought of bodies falling under his gun or his knife. And now he knew the two men within him. One was the man he wanted to be, but for now he had to be the other.

11

He would find Marie—dead or alive—and if she was dead he would kill, kill, and *kill again*! Whoever it was would never get away from him. Not from Jason Bourne.

He went downstairs, sat down at his desk, and tried to think clearly. The telephone rang, loud in the silence. He picked it up, holding the receiver tightly. "Yes?"

"This is the air operator. I have a radio call from an airplane in flight, for a Mr. Webb. Are you Mr. Webb, sir?"

"Yes."

And then the world he knew blew up in a thousand broken mirrors.

"David!"

"*Marie?*"

"Don't worry, darling!" She was trying not to shout but could not stop herself.

"Are you all right? The note said you were hurt—wounded!"

"I'm all right. A few scratches, that's all."

"Where are you?"

"Over the ocean. They're letting me speak to you so you'll know I'm alive. A man wants to talk to you, David. Listen to him, but not in anger – can you *understand* that?"

"All right. Yes, all right. I understand."

The man's voice came on the line—somebody who had been taught English by an Englishman, or had lived in the UK, but was obviously Chinese. "We do not want to harm your wife, Mr. Webb, but if it is necessary, it will be unavoidable."

"I wouldn't if I were you."

"You took something of great value from a man."

"What's your proof?"

"You were seen. A tall man who stayed in the shadows and raced through the hotel with the movements of a mountain cat."

"Then I wasn't really seen, was I? And that's not really

surprising, because I was thousands of kilometers away."

"In these days of fast airplanes, what is distance? Get to the Regent Hotel in Kowloon. Use any name you like, but ask for Suite 690. Be there by the end of the week."

"I'll be there. Put my wife back on the line."

The line went silent.

Chapter 4   Hong Kong

The mist rose above Victoria Harbour as the large jet circled for the final approach to Kai Tak airport. As the plane lost height, the skyscrapers on the island on Hong Kong shone in the first light of the morning sun. Webb studied the scene below. Down there somewhere was Marie.

He had phoned the Regent Hotel in Kowloon from Dulles airport requesting a room for a week in the name of Howard Cruett, the name on one of his three false passports. He had added, "I believe arrangements were made for me to have Suite 690, if it is available."

The suite would be available. But who had made it available?

"I've changed my mind," Webb said when he arrived at the counter of the Regent Hotel. "I don't want a suite. I'd prefer something smaller; a single or a double room."

"But the arrangements have been made, Mr. Cruett," replied the confused receptionist.

"Who made them?"

The young Chinese man looked down at a sheet of paper. "This was signed by the assistant manager, Mr. Liang."

"Then I should speak to Mr. Liang, shouldn't I?"

"I'm afraid it will be necessary. I'm not sure there's anything else available. I will go and find him."

The man walked rapidly across the crowded floor and

returned a few minutes later, with an older man.

The older man approached and said, "I am Liang. May I be of service?"

"Well, as I said, I prefer a single or a double room, not a suite."

"You specifically mentioned Suite 690, sir."

"I realize that and I apologize. I wasn't thinking clearly. But since you have no other rooms, I'll find somewhere myself."

"That will not be necessary. Arrangements can be made."

"But your man said—"

"He is not the assistant manager of the Regent, sir."

"My screen shows no free rooms," protested the young man.

Liang looked at him and, while smiling, spoke angrily in Chinese. Every word was understood by Webb. "Do not offer information in my presence unless I ask you! Now give this fool Room 200. It is reserved for another guest." He turned to Webb. "It is a very pleasant room with a view of the harbor, Mr. Cruett. If there is anything else you need, contact me."

"Thank you. It was a long and tiring flight, so I'll ask the operator to stop all calls until dinner-time."

"Oh?" Liang looked like a frightened man. "But surely if there is an emergency—"

"There's nothing that can't wait. Thank you, Mr. Liang."

"Thank you, Mr. Cruett." The assistant manager bowed, turned quickly, and headed back to his office.

Do the unexpected. Confuse the enemy. Jason Bourne.

"You have been very helpful," said Webb to the receptionist. He took out an American twenty-dollar bill and shook hands, the bill hidden. "When does Mr. Liang leave for the day?"

The young man looked quickly around. "You are most kind, sir. Mr. Liang leaves his office every day at five o'clock."

"Thank you," said Webb. "My key, please."

Up in his room, David Webb sat in the chair by the window looking across the harbor at the island of Hong Kong. Names

14

came to him with memories—Causeway Bay, Wanchai, Repulse Bay, Aberdeen, and finally, so clear in the distance, Victoria Peak with its view of the whole colony.

Marie was out there! He had to find her!

Webb reached for the notebook and pencil next to the phone on the bedside table. He wrote a shopping list, pulled off the page, and reached for his jacket.

It was ten minutes past noon when he returned with a number of thin plastic bags. In them there was a dark, lightweight raincoat and a dark hat, a pair of gray sports shoes, black pants, and a sweater, also black. These were the clothes he would wear at night. There were other things: some strong wire, an ice pick, and a sharp hunting knife. These were the silent weapons he would carry night and day. One more remained to be found.

As he examined the things he had bought, he noticed a tiny, flashing light. It was the message signal on the telephone. A *message* was not a call, he thought. He went to the table, picked up the phone, and pressed a button.

"Yes, Mr. Cruett," said the operator.

"There's a message for me?" he asked.

"Yes, sir. Mr. Liang has been trying to reach you—"

"I thought my instructions were clear," interrupted Webb. "I would receive no calls until I told the operator I wanted them."

"Yes, sir, but Mr. Liang is the assistant manager. He tells us it is most urgent. He has been calling you every few minutes for the past hour. I am ringing him now, sir."

Webb hung up the phone. He was not ready for Liang, or more accurately, Liang was not ready for him. Liang was possibly very frightened, because he had failed to place Webb in a suite where the enemy could listen to every word. But this was not good enough. Webb wanted Liang in total terror.

He took the clothes from the bed and put them into two drawers. He pushed the wire in among them and put the hunting knife in his jacket pocket. He looked down at the ice pick and suddenly had a thought: a frightened man would feel terror at an unexpected sight. Webb picked up a towel, reached down for the ice pick, and wiped the handle clean. Holding the pick in the cloth he walked into the small entrance hall of his room, judged the eye level, and stuck the pick into the white wall opposite the door. The telephone rang, then rang again steadily. Webb let himself out and ran down the passage toward the elevators. He went around the corner and watched.

He had not miscalculated. The doors of the middle elevator slid apart and Liang raced to the door of Webb's room. Webb could see him ringing the bell repeatedly, finally knocking on the door many times. Then he stopped and put his ear to the wood. Satisfied, he reached into his pocket and took out a ring of keys. Webb moved his head back out of sight as the assistant manager turned to look up and down the passage while putting a key into the lock. Webb did not have to see; he only wanted to hear.

He had not long to wait. A frightened cry was followed by the loud crash of the door. The ice pick had had its effect. Webb heard Liang run back to the elevator, breathing deeply as he repeatedly pressed his finger against the elevator button. Finally a bell rang and the metal doors of the elevator opened. The assistant manager rushed inside.

Webb walked down the passage to his room. He let himself inside, picked up the phone, and arranged for a Daimler car with the hotel's most experienced driver to be ready for him in ten minutes, behind the hotel. One of the hotel's employees would be standing by the car and would receive two hundred American dollars to keep the arrangement secret. There would be no individual's name given to the rental and Mr. Cruett could use a service elevator to the Regent's lower level.

The money paid, Webb climbed into the back seat of the Daimler and looked at the uniformed, middle-aged driver.

"Welcome, sir! My name is Pak-fei. You tell me where you want to go, and I take you."

Webb answered in Chinese, to show he was not simply a visitor. "But as I haven't been here in years, I want to get to know the place again. How about the normal tour of the island and then a quick trip through Kowloon? And now let's speak English."

"Ahh! Your Chinese is very good—very high class. I shall try to provide excellent service!"

He did, and the names and memories that had come to Webb in the hotel room were made more real. He knew the Central District and the tall buildings of the banks of Hong Kong. He had walked through the colorful streets of Wanchai. He recognized the road to Aberdeen and had swum in the crowded waters of Repulse Bay. He had seen it all, knew it all, but he could remember nothing of what had happened to him there ...

He looked at his watch. They had been driving for nearly two hours. There was a last stop to make on the island and then he would put Pak-fei to the test.

"Go back to the Central District," he said. "I have business at one of the banks. You can wait for me."

A large amount of money was a passport to free movement, and Webb needed to move quickly.

Back in the car, he leaned forward, resting his left hand on the soft cloth of the front seat. He held out an American hundred-dollar bill. "Pak-fei," he said, "I need a gun."

Slowly, the driver's head turned. He looked at the bill, then turned further to look at Webb. "Kowloon," he answered. "In Mongkok." He took the hundred dollars.

♦

At 5:02 an obviously worried Liang walked rapidly out of the glass doors of the Regent Hotel. He turned to his left and hurried along the sidewalk. Webb watched him from across the

17

street and followed as Liang moved toward the harbor.

The assistant manager stopped beside a public telephone and reached in his pocket for change. Suddenly, commanded by an inner voice, Webb knew that he could not allow that call. When it was made, *he* had to make it. The control had to be in his hands.

He began running, heading straight toward the pay phone. The assistant manager had just finished ringing a number.

"Liang!" shouted Webb. "Get off that phone! If you want to live, hang up and get out of here!"

Liang spun around, his eyes wide with fear. "You!" he shouted, pressing his body against the white plastic shell of the pay phone. "No ... *no*! Not now! Not *here*!"

Gunfire suddenly filled the winds off the water. People screamed, dropping to the ground or racing in all directions away from the terror of sudden death.

"Aieee!" screamed Liang, diving to the ground as the bullets burst into the harbor wall and cracked in the air.

Webb lay beside the hotel manager, his hunting knife in his hand. Liang screamed again as Webb held the front of his shirt and pushed the blade up into the manager's chin, breaking the skin. "Give me the number! *Now*!"

"Don't do this to me! I swear I didn't know it was a trap."

"It's not a trap for me, Liang," said Webb. "It's for you!"

"*Me*? You're mad! Why *me*?"

"Because they know I'm here now, and you've seen me, you've talked to me. You made your phone call and they can't afford you any longer."

"That explains *nothing*!"

"Maybe my name will. It's Jason Bourne."

"Oh, my God ...!" whispered Liang, his face pale.

"You've seen me," said Webb. "You're dead."

"No, *no*!" Liang shook his head. "That *can't* be right! I don't know anybody—only the number. It is an empty office in the

18

New World Centre with a temporary telephone. *Please*! The number is 34-401! Do not *kill* me, Mr. Bourne!"

The gunfire stopped as suddenly as it had begun.

"The New World Centre's right above us, isn't it? One of those windows up there."

"Exactly!" Liang said, shaking in fear.

Webb got to his feet, prepared to throw himself down again at the first irregular flash of light from a window above on the left. The eyes of Jason Bourne were accurate and there was nothing.

He made his call from a phone on Nathan Road.

"Hello," said a male voice, in Chinese.

"It's Bourne and I'll speak English. Where's my wife?"

Silence. Then, "I don't have this information."

"Then I'll talk to somebody who has it. *Now*!"

"You'll meet others who know more. Call 52-653."

Webb pressed down the telephone bar, disconnecting the line. He waited three seconds, let it go, and touched the buttons.

"*Wei*⋆?"

"This is Bourne. Put my wife on the line."

"As you wish."

Silence. Then, "David?"

"Are you all *right*?" shouted Webb.

"Yes, just tired, my darling. Are *you* all right—"

"Have they hurt you—have they touched you?"

"No, David, they've been quite kind, actually. You mustn't worry about me, darling. We'll be together soon, they've promised me that. It'll be like Paris, David. Remember Paris, when I thought I'd lost you? But you came to me and we both knew where to go. That lovely street with the row of green trees, my favorite tree—"

"That will be all, Mrs. Webb," a male voice interrupted, and

⋆ Wei?: the Chinese for "Hello?"

19

then gave an order: "Take her away."

"If you harm her in any way, you'll regret it for the rest of your short life," said Webb icily. "I swear to *God* I'll find you."

"You heard your wife. She has been treated well."

"Something's wrong with her."

"It is only her nerves, Mr. Bourne. And she *was* telling you something, no doubt trying to describe where she is, but the information will be useless to you. She is on the way to another apartment. A great taipan wants to meet you."

"Yao Ming?"

"Like you, he uses several names. Maybe you can reach an agreement."

"Either we do or he's dead. And so are you. Now, where can I meet Yao Ming?"

Chapter 5 The Taipan

Kowloon Walled City had no wall around it. Standing apart from the neighboring buildings, it rose to fourteen floors—buildings with more buildings piled on top. Legally, it belonged to the People's Republic of China, a part of the colony that was never British. In fact, neither Chinese nor British law had effect there. The police of both countries stayed away, as should outsiders.

Below ground level, narrow streets crossed beneath the buildings. Beggars competed with drug dealers in the light from bulbs that hung from wires running along the stone walls. The air smelled of decay.

Near the entrance to the market, a woman sat on a low wooden chair, her thick legs parted, skinning snakes. Her dark eyes concentrated on each moving creature in her hands.

Coming around the corner at the opposite end of the market, a poorly-dressed man turned into the busy street. He was dressed in a cheap, loose-fitting brown suit, the pants too wide and the jacket too large. A soft hat, black and unmistakably Chinese, threw a shadow over his face. He walked slowly, stopping in front of tables and examining the things on sale. Bent over, he looked like a man who worked in the fields or on the boats. He looked, in fact, like many of the men in the market.

The man approached the snake seller. "Where is the great one?" he said.

"You are early."

"I was told to come quickly. Do you question the taipan's instructions?"

"Go down the steps behind me and take the first street to the left. A woman will be standing fifteen, twenty meters down. She is waiting for you."

Remaining bent, Bourne bowed and moved away through the crowd. He made his way to the steps and went further down into the Walled City. The taipan's men would be moving into place.

The woman was walking into position. Several meters behind her a man spoke into a hand-held radio. Bourne stopped and turned to face the wall. A second Chinese man approached and passed him, a small middle-aged man in a dark business suit and shiny shoes. He was no citizen of the Walled City.

Bourne studied the irregular row of staircases. The man had to come from one of them. In one of the apartments above, a taipan was waiting for his visitor. Bourne had to find out which staircase and on what level.

Bourne moved forward and spoke to the woman. "I've been looking for you," he said.

"You are the *man*?"

"I am."

"I will take you to the taipan."

"No. You just have to tell me which staircase, which level. They're new instructions, given by the taipan." Bourne reached into his pocket and pulled out some folded bills. "He told me to give you extra money if you cooperated with me."

The woman looked at the money and at Bourne's face. "Over there," she said suddenly. "The third staircase, the second level."

"Besides the man with the radio, how many others work for the taipan? Quickly."

"Three others, also with radios," said the woman.

"Here, take it and leave," Bourne said.

Bourne moved back to the market. He found the first guard talking to a fish seller. The crowd around him was noisy. Bourne rushed forward and pushed him over. In the confusion that followed he pulled the guard to one side, and hit the base of the man's throat and then the back of the neck with the edge of his open hand. He dragged the unconscious man across the sidewalk, apologizing to the crowd in Chinese for his drunken friend. He dropped the guard in a corner, took the radio, and broke it.

The other two guards were just as easy to find and, for Bourne, as easy to deal with. The small middle-aged Chinese man in the expensive suit was now rushing around, trying to find his men. Bourne moved ahead of him, then turned suddenly and hit him in the stomach. As the man folded over, Bourne hit him with an open hand across the neck. He carried him to a dark corner.

Racing down the steps and into the street, he reached the staircase and pulled out the gun he had bought in Mongkok. He climbed to the second level and paused outside the door, then lifted his left leg and crashed it into the thin wood.

The door broke open. He jumped through, his weapon held out.

Three men faced him, each with a gun aimed at his head. Behind them was a large Chinese man in a white suit.

He had lost. Bourne had miscalculated and David Webb would die. Worse, he knew that Marie's death would soon follow.

"Welcome, Mr. Bourne," said the large man, sitting down. "Please put your gun on the floor and push it away from you."

Bourne did as he was told. "You expected me, didn't you?"

"We didn't know what to expect. Are my people dead?"

"No. They're hurt and unconscious, not dead."

"Interesting. You thought I was alone here?"

"I was told you had your head man and three others, not six."

"These men came early. So you thought you could take me and exchange me for your wife?"

"Let her go. She can't hurt you. Kill me, but let her go."

The banker ordered two of the guards to leave the room. They bowed and left quickly. "This man will remain," he said. "He doesn't speak or understand English. Now please sit down."

Bourne walked over to the chair. "I didn't kill your wife," he said. "Or the man who was with her."

"I know that, Mr. Webb."

"You *what*?" Webb stood up from the chair and the guard took a rapid step forward, his gun leveled.

"Sit down," repeated the banker.

"You knew it wasn't me and still you've *done* this to us!" Bourne said, sitting down.

"Yes. Because you are the true Jason Bourne. That's why you are here, why your wife is my prisoner, and will remain so until you do what I ask of you."

"And what is that?" asked Bourne.

"There is a new Jason Bourne," began the taipan. "He kills my people, destroys my goods, threatens other taipans with death if they do business with me. He is paid by my enemies here in Hong Kong and Macao, and in the People's Republic itself." The taipan leaned forward. "Bring him to me, Jason Bourne." The banker breathed deeply, then added quietly, "Then, and only then, will you be reunited with your wife."

"But how do I find him?"

"Quite recently," the banker said, "five men were killed in a night club here in Kowloon. One of them was a banker—like myself, a taipan—as well as three others. I've never found out

23

who they were. The government has kept their names secret."

"But you know who the fifth man was?"

"He worked for me. He took my place at that meeting. If I'd been there myself, this Jason Bourne would have killed me. This is where you will start." The banker reached into his vest pocket and took out a sheet of paper. "This has the names of two of the known dead. There are also names and contact details of men who were enemies of both—now my enemies."

Bourne took the sheet of paper. "If I manage to find and take this fool who calls himself Bourne, what do I do with him? Leave him on the steps outside here?"

"There's a phone number on the paper. It isn't listed anywhere and when you call, be prepared to deliver the impostor— alive—within minutes. If you or anybody else calls without that guarantee, I'll know you're trying to work out where the phone is. If that happens, your wife will be killed."

Swallowing, trying to keep his anger under control, Bourne spoke coldly. "The condition is understood. Now you understand mine. When and if I make that call, I'll want to speak to my wife—not within minutes but within seconds. If I don't, whoever's on the line will hear the gunshot and you'll know that your assassin is dead. You'll have thirty seconds."

"I understand. I think this conference has ended, Jason Bourne."

♦

High in the hills above the city in an area known as Victoria Peak are the large houses dating from Hong Kong's colonial period. One house was different from the others. At night very few lights burned in it and no sounds came from the window or the gardens. And at its gate there were American soldiers.

Inside the house, Edward McAllister sat behind a desk, studying the pages of a file. The phone rang. "Yes?" He listened and replied, "Send him in, of course." McAllister returned to the file in front of him. On the top of the page he was reading were the words repeated in the same position on each page: *Top Secret. People's Republic of China. Sheng Chouyang.*

The door opened and the large Lin Wen-zu of British Intelligence, Hong Kong, walked in, closed the door, and smiled at McAllister. "I'll be asking you to pay for the suit," he said. "White isn't my color."

"Of course," said McAllister, still reading.

"And also for the hospital treatment of four injured men."

"Bourne's very good at what he does—what he did."

"He's very dangerous, Edward. All the time I thought he'd make another move and blow that dirty room apart. The man's frightening. But I didn't come here tonight to tell you that—you know it already." McAllister closed the file and looked up. "The woman may be sick," Lin continued. "Her husband sensed it when he talked to her."

"You mean *seriously?*"

"It's possible—the doctor says it's possible."

"The *doctor?*"

"There was no point in alarming you. I called in one of our medical staff several days ago, a man I trust. She wasn't eating and complained of feeling sick. Since then she has got worse."

"What can we do?"

"The doctor thinks she should go to the hospital."

"She can't! Good *God*, it's out of the question."

The Intelligence officer rose from the chair. "Mr. McAllister, I'm afraid I must ask you: What happens to David Webb if his wife is seriously sick—or if she dies?

Chapter 6 Marie

"I need her medical history, as fast as you can provide it."

He's the English doctor who examined me. He's very polite, but *cold,*

25

and, I suspect, a very good doctor. That's fine.

"We'll get it for you. There are ways."

That's the big Chinese man. He's been nice to me. These are not bad people. This is a government operation.

Marie opened her eyes. The door was closed, the room empty, but she knew a guard was outside—she had heard the Chinese man giving instructions.

She sat up, then got off the bed and walked to the window. Outside it was night. She turned and looked around the room.

Study everything. You'll find something you can use. Jason's words, not David's. Then she saw it.

On some hospital beds—and this was one of them—there is a handle that raises or lowers the bed. David had spent many months in the hospital and Marie knew this type of bed. She removed the handle, then turned off the light in the room. She turned on the bathroom light, closing the door until little light showed.

She opened the door of the bedroom and looked at the guard.

"Come inside, quickly," she said. "I need to speak to you."

Marie pulled back the door, then moved behind it. The guard walked in, puzzled. Marie shut the door quickly. She could see the guard but he couldn't see her.

"Where are you, Mrs. ..."

He could not say anything more because Marie hit him over the head with the iron handle. The guard fell to the floor. She knelt down, took off his clothes and shoes, and put them on. Then she ran to the closet, picked up her own clothes, and went to the door. Opening it a little, she looked down the passage. There was nobody in sight. She ran down it to the EXIT sign.

Out in the hospital grounds, Marie ran into the parking lot and sat breathless in the shadows between two cars. She dropped her clothes and began searching the guard's pockets. She found a wallet and counted the money. There was around six hundred Hong Kong dollars, about one hundred American dollars. There

26

was also a credit card from a Kowloon bank. She removed the money and the card and changed into her own clothes, then ran out of the parking lot and into the street.

She walked for hours, stopping to eat at a fast food restaurant. From a street seller she bought flat shoes and a purse. She had forty-five American dollars left. It was not enough for a hotel room and she had no idea where to spend the night.

She passed a market that was closing. A young American couple were bargaining with the owner of a T-shirt stand.

"Excuse me," Marie said, speaking mainly to the girl. "It's most embarrassing, really, but my plane was a day late and I missed my tour into China. The hotel is full and I wondered—"

"You need a place to sleep?" interrupted the young man.

"Yes, I do. I don't have much money. I'm a schoolteacher."

"We can help you, can't we, Lacy?" he said.

"Of course. We're staying at the Chinese University of Hong Kong. It isn't a 5-star hotel but it's only three dollars a night."

"That would be fine," said Marie.

♦

Bourne met the first man on the taipan's list of enemies on one of the passenger boats that cross Victoria Harbour. The man knew nothing about how to contact the assassin, only that the assassin worked from Macao. He said this with Bourne's gun pointing at his stomach, so was probably telling the truth.

The second name belonged to the manager and owner of a restaurant in Causeway Bay. Bourne met him at a table.

"I have a silenced gun under the table. It's pointing between your legs," Bourne said. He quickly pulled up the weapon so it could be seen, then pushed it back into place.

"What do you want?" said the man, shaking with fear.

"Information. You've had contact with a man I want to find. The one for hire who calls himself Jason Bourne."

"*No!* It never happened."

The man's eyes moved away from Bourne's face.

"You're a liar," said Bourne quietly, pushing his right arm under the table as he leaned forward. "How did you make contact?"

"I had to meet a Frenchman in Macao."

"Who told you to do this?"

"I don't know. Everything is done by telephone. I do not know the callers and they tell me to expect instructions."

"How do they arrive? Somebody has to give them to you."

"Somebody who is no one, who is hired himself, will bring me an envelope. I will have ten thousand dollars for passing it on."

"How do you reach this Frenchman?"

"I go to Macao, to the Kam Pek casino. I go to table five and leave the telephone number of a Macao hotel and a name—not my own, naturally. I stay twenty-four hours in Macao. If he has not called by then, I have been turned down because the Frenchman has no time for me."

"Those are the rules?"

"Yes. I was turned down twice and the time I was accepted he did not appear for the meeting. I have never met him."

"I think I believe you," Bourne said.

"*Believe*, sir. I am only a messenger."

"You'll still walk with me to the door," Bourne told him. "I may believe you but I don't have to trust you."

♦

Marie made her way from the Chinese University to Kowloon and then crossed the harbor to Hong Kong Island and went to Asian House. The Canadian consulate was on the fourteenth floor. She took the elevator.

"I realize this will sound silly," she said to the woman at the desk, "but one of my mother's cousins is working here and I promised her that I'd say hello."

"That doesn't sound silly to me."

"It will when I tell you I've forgotten his name." Both women laughed. "Of course, we've never met, but it's important to the family back home."

The woman opened a drawer and took out a white file. "Here's a list of the people who work here. Why don't you sit down and look through it?"

"Thanks very much," said Marie, going to a chair.

On the twelfth page she found a name she knew. Catherine Staples. Marie had met her when Catherine worked in Ottawa. She hadn't got to know her very well, just four or five lunches, over a year ago, but she remembered her as good at her job.

"There isn't a name here that I recognize," Marie said, taking the file back to the desk. "I feel so stupid. I'll have to make a very embarrassing call to Vancouver and find out his name."

"Well, good luck with the call," said the woman.

Marie waited outside the building for over an hour before Catherine walked out and crossed the sidewalk. There was a consulate car waiting. She was climbing inside.

"No. *Wait!*" shouted Marie, crashing through the crowd, holding the door as Catherine was closing it.

"I beg your pardon?" cried Catherine, as the driver spun around in his seat, a gun appearing from nowhere.

"*Please*! It's *me*! Ottawa—we had lunch ..."

"*Marie*? Is that *you*?"

"Yes. I'm in trouble and I need your help."

"Get in," said Catherine Staples, moving over on the seat. "Put that thing away," she told the driver. "This is a friend of mine."

Chapter 7 The Frenchman

Sixty kilometers southwest of Hong Kong was the peninsula of

29

Macao, which was a Portuguese colony in name only. The real controls were in Beijing.

Bourne took the boat from Hong Kong and then a taxi to the Kam Pek casino. Inside, he sat down at the bar. He ordered a drink, speaking in Chinese, and when it came he gave the barman a generous tip in Hong Kong money. Then he pulled out a page from his notebook and wrote the telephone number of a Macao hotel.

"Would you do something for me?" Bourne said to the barman.

"What is it, sir?"

"Give this note to the dealer at table five. He's an old friend and I want him to know that I'm here." Bourne folded the note and held it up. "I'll pay you for your help."

"I'm happy to do this for you, sir."

Bourne watched. The dealer took the note, opened it quickly as the barman walked away, and pushed it beneath the table.

Hours passed, and Bourne moved from alcohol to tea to keep his head clear. Then a Chinese woman walked up to table five. The dealer gave her the folded note.

Bourne left the bar and followed the woman out of the casino. A bent old man approached the woman. Their bodies touched and she shouted at him while passing the note. Bourne pretended to be drunk and turned around, following the old man.

The next handover happened four blocks away. This time the man was younger. He was small but his body showed his strength. He paid the old man and walked across the street.

Bourne started to run. As the man passed a dark, narrow side street, he moved ahead. "The Frenchman!" he said in Chinese. "I have news from the Frenchman! *Hurry*!"

He spun into the side street, and the contact, shocked, followed him. From the shadows, Bourne took hold of the man and threw him down onto the ground.

The man stared up at Bourne. "*You*! It is *you*!" Then the

contact looked at him more carefully in the weak light. "No," he said, suddenly calm. "You are *not* him."

Without a warning move, the Chinese pushed his right leg out, moving his body off the sidewalk. He caught Bourne's left leg, following the blow with his left foot, striking into Bourne's stomach as he jumped to his feet, hands held out and stiff.

There followed a battle of animals, two trained assassins, each blow made with careful thought, each one able to kill if it landed with full force. Finally, height and weight and a reason beyond life itself gave victory to Bourne.

Bourne held the contact's neck with his arms, his left knee in the man's back, pushing him against the wall.

"You know what happens next!" he whispered slowly in Chinese. "One pull and your back breaks. It's not a pleasant way to die. And you don't *have* to die. You can live with more money than the Frenchman would ever pay you if you show me where the Frenchman and his assassin will be tomorrow night. Make your choice. *Now!*" Bourne put on more pressure.

"Yes, *yes!*" cried the contact. "I want to live, not die."

♦

Leaving Marie to rest in her apartment, Catherine Staples returned to the Canadian consulate. As there was no Canadian Intelligence Force operating in Hong Kong, foreign service officers used their own contacts. Catherine's was Ian Ballantyne, a retired British detective who had moved to Hong Kong to run the Intelligence section of the colony's police.

She called him, and the conversation surprised her. He said that McAllister had lied to Marie Webb and her husband in Maine. There was no taipan in Hong Kong named Yao Ming, and there had been no double murder involving a taipan's wife and a drug dealer at the Hotel Lisboa.

Catherine put the phone down and decided that there were

only two possibilities. This was either the most stupid operation she had ever heard of or a smart plan to involve David Webb in something he would not normally agree to.

♦

Havilland was talking to Lin Wen-zu in the walled garden of the United States consulate about Marie's disappearance when McAllister ran toward them.

"*Lin*! When Webb's wife took the call from her husband—the call you ended—what exactly did she say?"

"She began talking about a street in Paris where there was a row of trees—her favorite tree, I think she said."

"That's it!" said McAllister. "Her favorite tree! The maple tree, the maple *leaf*—from the Canadian flag! The Canadian consulate is their meeting place."

"The Canadian consulate," said Havilland to Lin Wen-zu. "Get me a list of everybody who works there."

♦

Bourne was across the border, in the hills fifteen kilometers north of the village of Gongbei. At the top of the next hill, just above the woods, they could see a campfire.

Bourne turned to his guide, the man he had fought with the night before. "You can leave now." He pulled some money from his pocket. "I'd rather go alone. One man has less chance of being seen than two." Bourne handed the guide the money. "It's all there. Ten thousand American dollars. Now get out of here. This is my business."

"And this is my gun," said the guide, handing a weapon to Bourne. "Use it if you must. It's fully loaded—nine bullets."

"You brought this across the *border*?"

"The guards were paid well. They let me bring *you* across—why should they worry about a gun?"

32

"Thank you," said Bourne.

He moved quietly through the trees toward the fire. A soldier, a gun on his waist, was standing roughly ten meters to the left. The man looked at his watch; the waiting had begun.

It lasted the better part of an hour and then it happened, slowly. A second figure appeared. He walked quietly out of the shadows and as he came Bourne's eyes opened wider in surprise. He was looking at a ghost of himself, or of himself some years before.

There was a crack in the distance and the man stopped, then spun away from the fire and dove to his right as the soldier dropped to the ground. Gunfire came from the woods and the killer rolled over on the grass, bullets thundering into the earth as he reached the darkness of the trees. The Chinese soldier was on one knee, firing wildly in the assassin's direction.

Three grenades were thrown, and the explosions were enormous. The Chinese soldier was dead, his gun blown away, as well as most of his body. A figure suddenly raced in from the left. He turned, saw Bourne, and fired at him. The assassin had turned back in the woods, hoping to trap and kill those who were trying to kill him. Bourne got to his feet and ran forward. *He could not let him get away!* He raced through the fires. The figure was running through the trees, only meters ahead of him.

Bourne jumped—Bourne against Bourne! He held the assassin's shoulders and his heels dug into the earth. They fell to the ground, Bourne's arm across the man's throat.

"*D'Anjou!* I am *d'Anjou! Medusa!* We were together in Tam Quan! You saved my life in Paris. You are Jason Bourne!"

Bourne stared at the face below him, the gray mustache and the silver hair, and remembered Tam Quan.

"If you give me back my throat," said the Frenchman, "I will tell you a story. I'm sure you have one to tell me."

The two men of Medusa sat on the ground and the Frenchman talked. "I didn't know what happened to you in Paris, whether

33

you won or lost, lived or died. But I knew that Jason Bourne was finished and that Washington would never say a word about it."

"Of course," said Bourne.

"So there was a place for an assassin here in Asia. There are men who will pay for the services of a man like Jason Bourne. I went to Singapore, and it didn't take long to find the right man. He is an Englishman, a former officer in the British Army who had too many bad experiences. One night he got drunk and killed seven people in London. He had been running from the police for nearly three years when I found him."

"He looks like me. Like I used to look."

"More now than he did. Surgery changed his face."

"So you found him, you changed him, you trained him. And now you want to kill him? Why?"

"Yes," said d'Anjou. "He broke away from me and began to accept contracts himself. With a new face and a new name, he wasn't afraid of the British police any more."

"But I found him through you, through your arrangements at the Kam Pek casino. Table five."

"He finds it convenient to use this method."

"So you called him here tonight to kill him? What made you so sure he would come?"

"Because we are in China, and I know he works for somebody in the government here."

"I heard that before," said Bourne, "and I still don't believe it."

"Five men were killed in a nightclub in Kowloon—"

"I know that."

"Four of them were meaningless. Not the fifth. He was the Vice-Premier of the Peoples' Republic."

"God! But why has nothing been said about it?"

"There were angry words between Hong Kong and Beijing, but nothing more. What, they wondered, was the Vice-Premier doing in Kowloon? But my assassin must be killed before he accepts another contract that could lead to serious trouble."

"Sorry, not killed. He must be taken to somebody else."

"Tell me—why?"

"Because my wife was kidnapped and is in Hong Kong. To get her back I have to deliver your man. And now I'm one step closer because you're going to help me. If you don't—"

"Threats are unnecessary," interrupted the Frenchman. "I know what you can do. We'll work together."

◆

The phone rang twice. There was a pause and then it rang again. It was the signal that Catherine was calling. Marie picked it up.

"Marie, I don't know how they found out, but they know I'm helping you. They followed me—I just got away from them. They'll be on the way to the apartment. You have to get out— *now*! My car's in the garage a block to your right as you leave the building. It's called Ming's; the sign's in red. Get there as quickly as you can! I'll meet you. *Hurry!*"

Marie tried not to give in to fear. She was dressed in Catherine's robe, having taken a long hot bath and washed her clothes. They were hanging over plastic chairs and still wet. And the cheap shoes had hurt her feet and walking was difficult. But she dared not walk, she had to run.

She dressed, the wet clothes sticking to her body, and found a pair of shoes in Catherine's closet. They were uncomfortable but softer than the ones she had bought.

Her red hair! She ran to the bathroom, found some hairpins, and fixed her hair to the top of her head. Then she found her foolish hat and put it on before leaving the apartment.

Avoid elevators whenever you can. They're traps. Jason Bourne. Zurich. Marie looked up and down the passage. She saw the fire-exit stair door and ran to it.

Out of breath, she ran into the short entrance hall, then slowed

35

to a walk among people entering and leaving the building. Outside she started running again. Her left shoe fell off. She stopped, bending down to put it back on. Suddenly a car shot out of the gates of a park across the wide street and drove at her. It turned hard. A man jumped out and raced toward her.

There was nothing else to do. Marie screamed, and screamed again, as the Chinese man approached and took her politely but firmly by the arm. People stopped and turned in the street.

"*Please, Mrs. ...!*" cried the Chinese man urgently. "No harm will come to you. Allow me to take you to my vehicle."

"*Help me!*" shouted Marie, as the surprised evening walkers gathered into a crowd. "This man's a thief. He stole my purse, my money! He's trying to take my jewelry!"

"Easy, friend," shouted a voice with an Australian accent as a man rushed forward. "Take your hand off the lady!"

"Please sir, this is a serious misunderstanding. The lady is in danger and she is wanted for questioning by the police."

"I don't see your uniform."

"Please let me show you my papers."

"That's what he said an hour ago when he attacked me in Garden Road!" shouted Marie. "People tried to help me then! He lied to everybody! Then he stole my purse!" Marie knew that none of this made sense. She could only hope for confusion, something that Jason had taught her to use.

"I'm not saying it again," shouted the Australian. "Take your hands off the lady!"

"Please, sir. I cannot do that. Other officials are on their way."

The Australian took the Chinese man by the shoulder, spinning him to his left. But as the Chinese man spun, his right foot swung around, crashing up into the Australian's stomach. The Australian fell to his knees.

"I'm asking you not to get *involved*, sir!"

"*Are you?*" The angry Australian got up, throwing his body

36

at the Chinese man, hitting him again and again. The crowd shouted—and Marie's arm was *free*! Then three police cars and an ambulance arrived at high speed.

Marie ran through the crowd toward the red sign half a block away. The shoes had fallen off her feet, which hurt as she ran. She could not allow herself to think about it. She had to run, *run*, *get away*! Then she heard a loud voice over the noise of the crowd. She remembered the big Chinese man from the hospital.

"Mrs. *Webb*! Mrs. Webb, I *beg you! Stop*! We intend no harm! You'll be told *everything*! Please, *stop*!"

Told everything! thought Marie. Told lies and more lies!

She kept running. Then she saw Catherine, waving at her from the window of a small car.

"Get in!" Catherine shouted.

Marie jumped into the front seat as Catherine drove quickly away, half on the sidewalk, then swung into a break in the traffic.

Chapter 8 Kai Tak Airport

Late the next morning, with Marie safely hidden away in a friend's flat, Catherine Staples drove to the house on Victoria Peak and demanded to see Ambassador Havilland. Lin Wen-zu showed her into his office. Havilland and McAllister stood up as she entered. They could see that she was very angry.

"You've gone too far, Havilland," said Catherine, her voice icy.

"Not far enough where you're concerned, Mrs. Staples ..."

Catherine looked at the undersecretary of state. "So this is the liar called McAllister."

"You're very tiring," said the undersecretary.

"And you're the little rat who does another man's dirty work. I've heard it all and it's all awful. But it was all planned" —Catherine turned her head toward Havilland— "by somebody

37

higher up. Who gave *you* the right to play *God*? *Any* of you? Do you know what you've done to those two people out there? Do you know what you've asked of them?"

"We know," said the ambassador simply. "I know."

"She knows, too, despite the fact that I couldn't bear to tell her. But I will. You and your lies! A taipan's wife murdered in Macao—lies! Well, understand this. I'm bringing her into the consulate under the protection of my government. You and your people have lied to and tricked a Canadian citizen into a highly dangerous operation. Who the hell do you think you are?"

"My dear woman!" shouted the ambassador, losing control in his sudden anger. "Make all the threats you like, but you will listen to me! And if, after that, you wish to start a war, you do that! My days are coming to an end, but not those of millions of others. I'd like to do what I can to keep those people alive. But you may disagree, so have your war, dear lady! And, by God, you live with what happens!"

Catherine sat down in a chair facing the two men. They looked at each other, then returned to their seats.

"I'm waiting," Catherine said. "Say what you have to say."

"Very well," said Ambassador Havilland. He described Sheng's plans. She demanded proof. By 2:15 she had twice read the State Department's long and top secret report on Sheng Chouyang, but she continued to object, as the accuracy of the document could not be proved. At 3:30 she was taken to the radio room and given a set of "facts" by a man named Reilly of the National Security Council in Washington.

"You're only a voice, Mr. Reilly," Staples said. "How do I know you're not somewhere in Hong Kong?"

At that moment another voice spoke, a voice that Catherine and the world knew very well. "This is the President of the United States, Mrs. Staples. If you doubt that, I suggest you call your consulate. Ask them to reach the White House by diplomatic phone and check. I'll wait. At the moment I have nothing better to do—nothing more important."

Shaking her head and closing her eyes for a few seconds, Catherine answered quietly, "I believe you, Mr. President."

"Forget about me—believe what you've heard. It's the truth. Mrs. Staples, we need you."

"I'm beginning to understand, Mr. President. Thank you."

♦

The roofs of Kai Tak airport were covered with police, as were the gates and the baggage areas. Outside, powerful lights were joined by sharper searchlights checking every moving vehicle, every piece of ground. Television crews and interviewers waited. And then the totally unexpected happened as a sudden rainstorm swept over the colony from the darkness in the west.

"The impostor has good luck, doesn't he?" said d'Anjou.

He and Bourne were wearing Hong Kong Police uniforms, supplied by the Frenchman, and they marched with a large group of police toward one of the enormous repair buildings.

"Not luck," replied Bourne. "He studied the weather reports. Every airport has them."

"But he could not know the arrival time of the Chinese plane. They are often hours late, usually hours late."

"But not days, not usually. When did the police get information about the assassination attempt?"

"Around eleven o'clock this morning."

"When we get to the building, I want to move away. Can your false papers make it possible?"

"I am an officer in the Hong Kong Police."

"You don't sound British."

"Who would know that out here at Kai Tak? And you are an Israeli Secret Service officer sent to us in an exchange program."

"Good God, I don't speak Hebrew!"

"Who here does? Speak English. Most Israelis do. You'll be free to move around."

"I'll have to be," said Jason Bourne. "If it's your assassin, I want him before anybody else sees him! Here! Now!"

The big jet dropped onto the runway and Bourne walked quickly into the roped-off area, looking for a man who looked like himself. There were about two dozen men with cameras, and he went from one photographer to the next, making sure that each man could not be the killer. *Nothing*! No one! He had to *find* him, *take* him! Before anybody else found him. The assassination wasn't important to him. Nothing mattered except Marie.

The enormous 747 of the People's Republic of China came into view, its engines shutting down as it reached its position. The doors opened and the two leaders of the British and Chinese groups came out together. They waved and walked down the metal stairs, one in a business suit, the other in the plain uniform of the People's Army. The leaders approached the microphones and their voices came through the speakers. Now Bourne did feel fear rise within him. If the assassin managed to kill either or both leaders, it might start a war.

Bourne moved out beyond the ropes to get a better view. He studied the television crews—their looks, their eyes, their equipment. If the assassin was among them, which one *was* he?

The watching people clapped. The short speeches had ended, signaled by the arrival of the official cars, each with motorcyclists driving up between them and the roped-off crowd of journalists and photographers. It was the moment. If anything was going to happen, it would happen now. If a bomb was going to be exploded, it would have to be placed *now*!

A few meters to his left he saw a police officer, a tall man whose eyes were moving as quickly as his own. Bourne leaned toward the man and spoke in Chinese while holding out his pass.

"I'm the man from Israel. Can you get me in?" Bourne said.

"I haven't got time to show papers!'

"Yes, I was told about you!" The officer led him through.

Bourne was now between the row of cars and the rope. He approached the leading car, using his flashlight to look underneath.

It *happened*, but Bourne was not sure what it was! His left shoulder touched another shoulder and the contact was electric. The man he had touched first fell forward then swung around. Bourne raised his flashlight to look.

Like a lightning strike, Bourne was staring at *himself*–but from years ago! The face was *his*! It was the *impostor*! The *assassin*!

The eyes that stared back at him also showed fear, but they were quicker than Bourne's. A stiff, flattened hand crashed into Bourne's throat, cutting off all speech and thought. He fell back, unable to scream, holding his neck as the assassin rushed past Bourne, and went under the rope.

Get him! Take him! ... *Marie*! Bourne got to his feet and jumped over the rope, running into the crowd, following the fallen bodies that had been knocked down by the killer.

"Stop ... *him*! Let me *through*!" Bourne said, with difficulty, but no one was listening. From somewhere near them a band was playing in the rain.

The path was closed! There were only people, people, *people*! The killer was gone!

Killer? The *kill*!

It was the car, the leading car with the flags of both countries! Somewhere in that car or beneath it was the bomb that would blow it to the skies, killing the leaders of both groups.

Bourne spun around, looking for somebody in charge. Twenty meters beyond the rope was an officer of the Kowloon police. Fixed to his belt was a radio. A *chance*! The cars had started to move slowly toward an unseen gate in the airport.

Bourne ran toward the Chinese officer. "Stop them!"

41

he shouted.

"What?" replied the surprised man, reaching for his gun.

"*Stop* them! The *cars*! The one in *front*!"

"What are you talking about? Who are you?"

"I'm the one from Israel!" Bourne shouted. "*Listen* to me! Get everybody out of that car! It's going to blow up! *Now*!"

Through the rain the officer looked up into Bourne's eyes, then nodded once and pulled the radio from his belt. "This is an emergency! Put me through to Red Star One. *Immediately*!"

"*All* the cars!" interrupted Bourne. "Tell them to drive away!"

"Change!" cried the police officer. "Put me through to all vehicles!" And with his voice tense but controlled, the Chinese officer spoke clearly. "This is Colony Five and we have an emergency. With me is the man from Israel and I pass on his instructions. Red Star One must stop now and you must order everybody out of the vehicle, instructing them to run for cover. All other cars are to turn to the left toward the center of the field, away from Red Star One. *Immediately*!"

Shocked, the crowds watched as in the distance the engine sounds increased. Five cars swung out of position, racing into the outer darkness of the airport. The first car came to a stop; the doors opened and men jumped out, running in all directions.

Eight seconds later it happened. The car called Red Star One exploded fifteen meters from the open gate. Flaming metal and broken glass twisted up into the rain and the band music stopped.

Chapter 9   Beijing

The small motor boat rose and fell on the rough sea. It was dark and heavy rain was falling. D'Anjou held a flashlight up to his chest, and for a moment a dark blue flash lit up the window. Seconds later they saw a blue flash from the island's shore and d'Anjou turned the small boat toward it. Within minutes the boat touched sand. The Frenchman pushed the stick down, lifting the motor out of the water, as Bourne jumped out, took hold of the rope, and began pulling the small boat up the beach.

He was surprised by the figure suddenly next to him, holding the rope. "Four hands are better than two," shouted the stranger, a Chinese man. He spoke English with an American accent.

"You're the *contact*?" shouted Bourne, puzzled.

"That's such a foolish term!" replied the man, shouting back. "I'm just a friend!"

Five minutes later the three men sat in a simple shelter around a small fire.

"Who the hell are you?" asked Jason Bourne.

"I will leave that to your imagination. You could start with the University of Southern California. Back in the 1960s. Then graduate studies at Berkeley."

"My friend here is the perfect contact," said d'Anjou. "He works for anybody if the money is right. I respect him for that."

"So why are we here?" Bourne asked.

"I have information," the officer said. "You'll want it, I promise you. The price is one thousand American dollars."

"You expect me to give you a thousand dollars because you promise me I'll want the information?" d'Anjou said.

"You are so French," said the officer, shaking his head. "Very well, it is about your student, the one who no longer follows his master but instead works for himself."

"The *assassin*?"

"*Pay* him!" ordered Bourne, staring at the Chinese officer.

D'Anjou took some bills out of his money belt. He held them out. "Three thousand for tonight and one for this new information."

"Your former student has been called to Beijing," said the officer, taking the money.

"You're sure of that?" said Bourne.

43

"The man I paid for the information is sure."

Bourne looked at the Chinese officer. "Get us into Beijing," he said. "The airport, the earliest flight. You'll be rich, I promise."

"You think you can take him in *China*?" d'Anjou asked.

"Where else would he least expect a trap?"

"*Madness*! You *are* mad!"

"Make the arrangements," Bourne ordered the Chinese officer. "The first flight out of Kai Tak. When I have the tickets, I'll hand over fifty thousand American dollars to whoever gives them to me. Send somebody you can trust."

"Fifty *thousand* …?" The Chinese officer stared at Bourne.

♦

The skies over Beijing were not clear; the dust had traveled on the winds from the North China plains.

Bourne and d'Anjou went through customs with little effort, the way made easier because they spoke Chinese well. The official accepted without question the story of two college teachers of Chinese on a vacation.

"Stay by the window," Bourne said to d'Anjou. "There's another twelve minutes before the next plane is due from Kai Tak. I'm going to buy us both a present."

Bourne returned with two long, thin, brightly-colored boxes. He removed the top of one of them. Inside was a sharp, narrow metal letter-opener, with Chinese characters along the handle.

"Take it," said Bourne. "Put it in your belt."

The waiting continued as plane after plane arrived. No one looked possible until an older man walked by.

"*That* one!" cried d'Anjou.

"The one with a stick?" asked Bourne.

"His old clothes cannot hide his shoulders!" said d'Anjou. "The gray hair is too new and the dark glasses are too wide. Like us, he is tired. He had to get here and he is being careless."

44

"He's heading for the hotel." said Bourne. "Stay back here—I'll follow him. If he saw you, he'd run and we could lose him."

Carrying his flight bag, Bourne joined the line of passengers heading into the hotel. The crowd at the counter grew and Bourne was eight people behind the killer in the second line. The assassin reached the front. He showed his papers to the woman there, and signed the book. Then he walked slowly toward the elevators on the right. Six minutes later Bourne faced the same woman.

"Can I have a room?" he said in Chinese. "It was a sudden trip and I have no place to stay. Just for the night."

"You speak our language very well," said the woman. "I'll see what I can do."

"Also, I have a friend with me. We can share a room."

The woman's fingers went through the file cards. "Here," she said. "On the second floor. It's small but it's all we have."

"We'll take it," said Bourne. He took the room key and joined d'Anjou at the entrance.

"What happens now?" asked the Frenchman.

"He has to stay out of sight. He'll remain in his room waiting for a call giving him his instructions." They walked through a glass door and headed to the left of the long counter. Bourne continued, speaking rapidly. "Kai Tak didn't work last night, so he has to consider another possibility. He knows that whoever discovered the explosives under the car saw him and can kill him. So he has to make sure that his employer is alone when they meet." They found a staircase and started climbing. "And his clothes," Bourne continued. "He'll change them. He can't appear as he *was* and he can't appear as he *is*."

"So what do we do?" asked d'Anjou.

"Sooner or later he has to leave the hotel. We'll leave our bags in the room and wait across the street."

"Let's hope it's sooner," said d'Anjou.

◆

Marie woke with the first light after a sleep filled with bad dreams. Catherine had telephoned her late last night, only to say that several unusual things had happened. Marie should stay where she was and wait for things to develop. "I'll call you early in the morning, my dear." Staples had hung up.

By ten o'clock she had not called and Marie was worried. And then the phone rang. It was the beginning of real fear.

"Marie?"

"Catherine, are you all *right*?"

"Yes, of course."

"You said 'early in the morning'! Why didn't you call before? I've been going out of my mind! Can you talk?"

"Yes, it's a public phone—"

"What's happened? What's *happening*?"

There was a short pause on the line. For a moment it seemed strange and Marie did not know why.

"I didn't call before because you need all the rest you can get. I can tell you that your husband is still alive. And I can tell you that he's very good at what he does—what he *did*."

"Catherine, you're not telling me anything."

"I'm driving out to see you in a few minutes. The traffic's terrible, as usual, but it shouldn't take me more than an hour and a half, maybe two."

"Catherine, I want *answers*!"

"I'm bringing them to you—a few, at least. Rest, Marie, try to relax. Everything's going to be all right. I'll be there soon."

"All right."

Had it been Staples's voice? Marie wondered after hanging up. Catherine had told her nothing after admitting she could talk freely over a public phone. It had been the voice of a diplomat, not a friend.

She moved around unsteadily, gathering the clothes they had bought for her when they had reached Tuen Mun, a new city west of Kowloon, the previous night. Before this Staples had taken her to a doctor who had worked on her feet, putting on bandages and suggesting soft shoes if she had to do any walking in the next few days.

Marie walked to the window, looking at the world outside. It was not a world she knew. She was alone, and that loneliness was driving her crazy.

Then she saw Catherine! She was standing with a man by a gray car, their heads turned, watching three *other* men ten meters behind them by a second car. All five were very obvious; they were like no other people in the street. They were Westerners among Chinese, strangers in an unfamiliar place. Three of the men had very short hair … soldiers. *American soldiers!*

The man with Catherine, whose hair was longer, was talking rapidly, one finger in the air … Marie *knew* him! It was the man from the State Department, the one who had come to see them in Maine! It was *McAllister!*

Suddenly, the two soldiers by the second car crossed the street and separated. The one standing with Catherine talked quickly with McAllister, then ran to his right, pulling a small hand-held radio from his pocket. Staples spoke to the undersecretary and looked up at the apartment. Marie spun away from the window.

It was a trap! Catherine Staples had been reached. She was not a friend; she was the *enemy!* Marie knew she had to move quickly. She took the white purse with the money Catherine had given her and ran out of the apartment.

Chapter 10 Tiananmen Square

Across the street from the hotel, d'Anjou said, "There's something happening."

"What do you mean?" Bourne said.

47

"Look at that van just past the bus over there."

Bourne looked across the street. The van was white and had dark windows. He read the Chinese characters on the door: the Jinshan Bird Reserve. "What about it?" he said.

"The man in the open window, the last window on this side. He's looking back at the entrance. He's also an army officer. Do bird reserves use army officers?"

"A bird reserve," said Bourne. "It's beautiful. So quiet, so peaceful. It's a great place to meet and organize things."

"But why is the officer here? Can't they just arrange to *meet* the impostor?"

"They can, but he'll want to change the arrangements so he's in control. He knows they might decide to kill him after the mess at Kai Tak, so he'll try to get away from that van."

"Things were simpler in Vietnam," the Frenchman said.

"We've got to separate but stay in sight. I'll go— "

"No need!" d'Anjou interrupted. "There he is!"

"Where?"

"The priest talking to the little girl," answered d'Anjou, staring at the crowd in front of the hotel's entrance. "One of the many ways I taught him to change his appearance. He had the black suit made for him in Hong Kong. I paid for it."

Bourne studied the man he wanted to capture. The assassin looked very different. Gray hair could be seen under his dark hat, thin steel glasses were low on the nose of his pale face. He smiled at the little girl and nodded to the mother. Anybody trying to find a killer in the crowd would look at him and walk past.

"Be ready to move!" said d'Anjou. "He's nearing the bus."

"It's full."

"That's the point—he'll be the last one on. Who refuses a priest in a hurry? One of my lessons, of course."

The Frenchman was right. As the door of the small, dirty bus began to close, the priest pushed his arm in. The door opened

48

again and the killer got inside.

"It's the express to Tiananmen Square," said d'Anjou. "I have the number."

"We have to find a taxi. Come on!"

♦

Marie left the apartment building by the fire escape and took a taxi. She changed to another on the way to Kowloon and walked a couple of blocks before choosing a hotel on Chatham Road. Its customers were both western and Chinese, mainly businessmen who could not afford to stay in a more expensive place. She took a single room under a false name, Penelope Austin.

In her room she sat on the edge of the bed and thought about who could help her. One name came to mind. Alex Conklin. He had been a close friend of David in Cambodia a long time ago. When David's first wife and children were killed by an enemy plane, he ran away to Saigon, his anger uncontrollable. It was Alex Conklin who found a place for him in the group of men they called Medusa, who did dangerous jobs behind enemy lines.

But later, when David lost his memory, Conklin believed the worst of his former friend because he needed to feel better than Webb; in his work with Medusa, Conklin's foot had been blown off by a bomb, and his fine overseas career had been cut short. So Conklin had twice tried to kill him.

Later, when he realized his mistake, Conklin had repeatedly tried to see David, to explain, to apologize, but David was not interested in his words.

Marie reached for the telephone. "I need the number of a person in Washington, D.C., in the United States," she said to the operator. "It's an emergency."

"There is a charge for overseas information—"

"Charge it," Marie interrupted. "It's urgent. I'll stay on the line."

"*Yes?*" said the voice, filled with sleep. "*Hello?*"

"Alex, it's Marie Webb."

"Where *are* you? Where are *both* of you? He *found* you!"

"You know about all of this? How do you know?"

"Mo Panov told me—David spoke to him before he flew out."

"I'm in Hong Kong—Kowloon, I guess. The Empress Hotel, under the name of Austin. So David spoke to Mo?"

"Yes. He and I have done our best to find out what's happening, without success. Marie, what *is* happening?"

Marie told him, including the fact that she thought it was a government operation, and about the help given by Catherine Staples that turned into a trap. "What can I *do*?" she said.

"Stay where you are," ordered Conklin. "I'll be on the earliest plane to Hong Kong. Don't go out of your room. Don't make any more calls. They're searching for you—they have to be. "

"David's *out* there, Alex! I'm frightened to death for him!"

"He was the best man in Medusa. I know. I saw."

"Yes, but what about his *mind*? What will happen to his mind?"

Conklin paused. "I'll bring Mo Panov with me. He won't refuse. Stay where you are, Marie. It's time we started to fight back."

♦

Bourne and d'Anjou arrived before the bus and watched as it stopped at the end of a line of others. Tourists were getting out, and the two men watched as the assassin in priest's clothes helped an old woman down to the sidewalk. He said goodbye, turned away, and walked around the back of the bus.

"Stay about ten meters behind me and watch me," said Bourne. "Do as I do. When I stop, you stop; when I turn, you turn. Be in a crowd. Go from one group to another, but make sure there are always people around you."

Bourne ran to the end of the bus and stopped. His priest was about fifty meters ahead, his dark suit easy to see in the sunlight. Crowds or no crowds, he was easy to follow. Bourne moved closer. Twenty meters, fifteen, ten ... He broke away from one crowd into another ... the black-suited priest was within reach. He could *take* him! *Marie*!

A soldier. The priest spoke to him. The army man nodded and pointed to his left. Bourne looked over, puzzled, and saw a short Chinese man carrying a government briefcase. He was standing at the foot of a wide stone staircase up to an enormous building. The Chinese letters over the doors said that it was the tomb of Chairman Mao. Two lines of tourists were moving up the steps. Suddenly, the tall assassin held the soldier's arm, moving the smaller army man in front of him. The officer's back bent; a weapon had been pushed into it.

The assassin and his prisoner walked steadily toward the man with the briefcase. The man was afraid to move, and again Bourne understood. These men were known to the killer; they were the center of the tight circle that led to the assassin's employer, and that employer was near here, obviously somewhere inside the building, and could not know what was happening outside.

Bourne knew he had to act. Quickly. He had to get inside Mao Zedong's tomb and watch, wait for the meeting to end. Bourne turned, looking for d'Anjou. The Frenchman was on the edge of a group of visitors. He nodded and stopped. Bourne crossed behind the assassin and his prisoner and walked through the crowd, up the right side of the staircase to a guard.

He spoke in polite Chinese. "High Officer, I'm most embarrassed! I have lost my group, which passed through here only minutes ago."

"You speak our language very well," said the guard. "Get in the back of the line on the steps."

"You've been most kind."

Bourne rushed up the steps, bending down behind the crowd,

51

his head turned to watch the assassin's progress, The impostor talked quietly to the man with the briefcase, still holding the soldier—but something was odd. The man with the briefcase nodded, but his eyes were not on the impostor, they were looking beyond him.

Bourne walked through the doors, as surprised as everybody else by the enormous white stone figure of a seated Mao. He followed his tour group into the second great hall. Facing them was a glass box holding the body of Chairman Mao Zedong, covered by a red flag.

The sound of people talking loudly came from the first hall, but it stopped as soon as it had begun. Bourne slipped behind a pillar, hidden in the darkness, and looked around the shining stone.

Then he felt frightened, because there was no group following his own! It was the last admitted—he was the last person admitted—before the heavy doors were closed. It was a trap!

Then he realized that from the *beginning* it was a trap. The information paid for on a rainy island, the nearly unobtainable airline tickets that had come so easily, the first sight of the assassin at the airport—a professional killer able to change his appearance much more if he wanted to. Then the priestly black suit, paid for by the impostor's creator—so easily noticed, so easily followed. All of it was a trap for him and d'Anjou!

Quickly Bourne looked around. The group was now moving toward the exit doors at the other end of the building. But they would be watched; everybody would be studied as they left.

The sound of feet. Over his right shoulder. Bourne spun to his left, pulling the metal letter-opener from his belt. A figure in army uniform cautiously passed by the wide pillar. He was no more than two meters away. In his hand was a gun, a silencer on the end of it.

Bourne struck, the fingers of his left hand held tightly over the man's mouth as he pushed the letter-opener into the soldier's neck, the blade cutting the throat. Bourne dropped his left hand, holding the gun, and swung the body around, leaving it in the dark shadows beside the right wall. He moved back against the wall and stood behind a pillar.

He had to get *out*! There was only one way and Bourne knew he had to do it. He moved his body around the pillar and waited.

It happened. The officer who was the assassin's "prisoner" walked in with the short man carrying his briefcase. The soldier held a radio at his side; he brought it up to speak and listen, then shook his head, placing the radio in his right-hand pocket and pulling out his gun. The other man nodded once, reached under his jacket, and also took out a gun. Each walked forward toward the glass box containing the remains of Mao Zedong, then separated, one to the left, one to the right.

Now! Bourne raised his weapon and fired. *Once*! *Twice*! The sounds were like coughs in the shadows as both men went down. Using the edges of his coat, Bourne took hold of the silencer and spun it off. He aimed at the glass box, firing again and again. The explosions filled the room, made louder by the stone walls, breaking the glass, the bullets hitting the body of Mao Zedong.

Alarms went off, bells deafened the ear, as soldiers, appearing at once from everywhere, raced in fear toward the broken box. The tourists rushed toward the back doors. Bourne joined them, crashing his way into the center of an inside line. Reaching the light of Tiananmen Square, he raced down the steps.

D'Anjou! Bourne ran to the right, going around the stone corner, then down the side of the building until he reached the front. Guards were doing their best to calm the excited crowds while trying to find out what had happened.

Bourne studied the place where he had last seen d'Anjou, then moved his eyes over the area within which the Frenchman might be seen. Nothing—no one who looked at all like him.

Suddenly, there was the sound of an engine far off on a road to Bourne's left. He turned and looked. A van with darkened windows was speeding toward the south gate of the square.

They had taken d'Anjou.

Chapter 11 Alexander Conklin

Morris Panov and Alexander Conklin left the gift shop in the Kowloon railroad station and headed for the escalator that led to the lower level. Mo was carrying a large toy bear and looked a little embarrassed.

"You'll be fine," Conklin said, when they reached the platform. "Just do as I said and come back here."

Panov shook his head doubtfully, but walked down to the end of the platform as the train from Lo Wu came into the station. He waited as hundreds of passengers poured out of the doors.

"You must be Harold," said a loud, high voice, as a tall figure, heavily made up under a soft hat and dressed in a gray skirt, came toward him. "I'd know you *anywhere*, darling."

"Nice to meet you. How's the kid?" Morris said, remembering his instructions.

"How's Alex?" said the suddenly male voice quietly. "I owe him and I pay my debts, but this is crazy. Has he gone mad?"

"I think you're all mad," said the surprised doctor.

"Quickly," said the strange figure. "They're coming. Give me the bear, and when I start running, move into the crowd and get out of here! Give it to me!"

Panov did as he was told, seeing several men breaking through the groups of passengers and moving closer. Suddenly, the heavily made-up man in women's clothes ran behind a pillar, kicked off his high heels, and raced into the crowd nearest the train, passing a Chinese man who tried to stop him. The other men followed him but were held back by the increasingly angry passengers, who began using suitcases and bags against them.

Morris Panov quickly joined the departing crowd and walked rapidly back to the escalator. He looked around for Conklin.

"Mo!"

Panov spun to his left. Conklin had moved partly around a pillar ten meters beyond the escalator. Panov moved toward him. He reached the pillar, slid behind it, and stopped in surprise.

At Conklin's feet lay a middle-aged man in a raincoat, with Conklin's wooden foot in the center of his back.

"I'd like you to meet Matthew Richards, doctor. Matt's been in the Far East for years. We first knew each other in Saigon."

"Please, Alex, let me up!" begged the man named Richards. "What the hell did you hit me with?"

"The shoe belonging to my missing foot. Heavy, isn't it? But I can't let you up until you answer my questions."

"I'm just a case officer, not the station chief."

"Imagine it, being trapped behind a pillar in a crowded train station by a man with one leg. They'll probably let you finish your career in Greenland."

"I don't *know* anything!"

"Who are the Chinese guys who tried to catch my friend?"

"Government. That's all I know—*honest!*"

"There was one big man," Conklin said. "Who is he, Matt?"

"I don't know … for sure." Conklin suddenly raised his wooden foot and hit Richards in the middle of his back. "*All right*! I've heard he's high up in British Intelligence."

"Very interesting," said Conklin. "So the British are involved, too. May I have your tie, doctor?" he asked as he began removing his own. "I need yours, too, Matt."

Two minutes later, Case Officer Richards lay behind the pillar, his feet and hands tied and his mouth gagged.

"We're safe," said Conklin, looking at the crowd beyond the

pillar. "They've all gone after our man."

"Who was she—*he*? I mean, he certainly wasn't a woman."

"I've used him before. He can run fast."

Panov stared at Conklin as they went up the escalator and walked toward Marie's hotel.

"That's probably the big man I saw in the hospital," said Marie, when they were all in her room. "His name is Lin Wen-zu. Catherine Staples told me he was with British Intelligence. He speaks English with a UK accent."

"It's odd," Conklin said. "I can understand that London would agree to a secret American operation, but not that British Intelligence would lend us their local people in a colony that the UK is still running."

"Why?" asked Panov.

"A couple of reasons. First, they don't really trust us. But, more important, why risk their people for an American undersecretary with no experience in this type of operation?"

"You mean McAllister?" said Marie.

"Yes, he's good with facts and figures but he couldn't run this sort of thing. So who is in charge?"

"Catherine said something to me," Marie said. "She spoke about a man who flew into Hong Kong, a former ambassador—somebody who was 'much more than a diplomat'."

"What was his name?"

"She didn't say."

Conklin looked at his watch. "It's time we met Catherine."

"She'll be watched, guarded!" Marie sat forward in her chair. "They'll think you both came over here because of me, that you reached me and I told you about her. They'll expect you to go after her. They'll be waiting for you. If they could do what they've already done, they could kill you!"

"No, they couldn't," said Conklin, getting up and walking toward the bedside telephone. "They're not good enough."

♦

"You're crazy," whispered Matthew Richards from behind the wheel of the small car parked across the street from Catherine Staples's apartment.

"You're not very grateful, Matt," said Alex Conklin, sitting next to the CIA man. "I didn't send in a report and I also let you start following me again."

"I'm so happy."

"So it was my old friend Havilland who came into town?"

"You didn't get that from me! It was in the papers I gave you."

"The house on Victoria Peak wasn't in the papers, Matt."

"That was an exchange. You're nice to me, I'm nice to you."

A car slowed down and stopped across the street in front of Staples's apartment building. A woman got out and, seeing her in the light of the street lights, Conklin knew who it was. Catherine Staples. She turned around and walked toward the thick glass doors of the entrance.

Suddenly, a long, black car moved quickly out of a space somewhere behind them and came to a stop beside Staples's car. Explosions thundered from the second vehicle. Glass broke in the street and across the sidewalk as the windows of the parked car were blown away, with the driver's head. The doors to the apartment building fell apart in bloody pieces as the body of Catherine Staples was hit by bullets.

Tires spinning, the black car raced away down the dark street.

"*Oh my God!*" shouted Richards.

"Get out of here," ordered Conklin.

"*Where*? My God, *where*?"

"Victoria Peak."

"Are you out of your *mind*?"

"No, but somebody else is. Havilland's been fooled. And he's going to hear it first from me. *Move!*"

57

Chapter 12   The Jinshan Bird Reserve

Bourne had one clue—words written on the side of the van outside the hotel: the Jinshan Bird Reserve. The reserve was a few kilometers outside Beijing. With another of his false passports, and helped by the fact that he spoke excellent Chinese, he rented a car and drove out of the city. At the side of the reserve he drove the car off the road between two trees, turned off the lights, and got out. Rapidly he broke branches to hide the car. It was dark but the moon was full. Perhaps something would happen tonight.

He took a bag from the car's trunk and began sorting through the tools he needed. He removed his jacket and white shirt and put on a black sweater. He fixed his hunting knife to the belt of his dark jacket and pushed the gun, with only a single bullet in it, below it on the other side. He rolled up a wire with a wooden handle at each end and pushed it down inside the right back pocket of his pants, then put a small flashlight in his front pocket. He placed a long, double string of large Chinese firecrackers, which was folded and held in place by a rubber band, into his left front pocket with three books of matches. He pushed a wire-cutter down into his left back pocket.

Finally, he reached for a wrapped pile of clothing that was rolled tightly. He centered it on his backbone, pulled the belt around his waist, and fixed it in place. He might never use the clothes but he could leave nothing to chance. He was too close.

He moved cautiously through the bushes to the fence. He took the flashlight from his pocket, flashing it twice to judge the height. It was high, at least four meters, and the top came out like a prison fence, with razor-wire wrapped around the parallel steel wires. The birds in the reserve were well-protected.

Bourne started to cut through the thick wire. Each piece took all the strength he had as he moved the cutter backward and forward until the metal broke free. Then, using his shoulder, his feet digging into the ground, he bent the square of wire through the fence. He went through and lay on the ground breathing heavily.

He rose to his knees, shook his head to clear it, and started toward the gate. It was seventy meters to his left.

Suddenly a vehicle arrived—a Russian Zia car—and circled into the parking lot. Six men got out and walked toward the path before disappearing into the darkness.

Three minutes later a second car drove through the gate and parked beside the Zia. Three men got out of the back while the driver and the front seat passenger talked. Seconds later the two men came out, and Bourne saw that the tall, thin passenger who moved like a cat, was the assassin.

Eighteen minutes later six cars were in place, the passengers joining the others somewhere in the dark forest. Finally, a covered truck drove through the gate, parking no more than ten meters from Bourne. Shocked, he watched as tied and gagged men and women were pushed out and fell rolling on the ground in pain. Then, just within the covered opening, a man was struggling, twisting his short, thin body and kicking at the two guards, who held him off and finally threw him down on the ground. It was a Westerner ... Bourne *froze*. It was *d'Anjou*! He could see that the Frenchman's face had been hit hard.

Move! Do something! What? *Medusa—we had signals*. What were they? Sticks, rocks ... *small stones*!

Bourne dropped to his knees. He picked up a handful of stones and threw them in the air over the heads of the prisoners. The sound as they fell on the roofs of several cars was largely hidden by the cries of pain from the prisoners, but d'Anjou heard it and slowly turned his head in Bourne's direction. Quickly, Bourne pushed the flat of his hand out—once, twice—and the Frenchman's eyes moved toward it. Bourne moved his head forward in the shadows. Their eyes made contact. D'Anjou nodded, then turned away.

Bourne counted the prisoners. There were two women and five men, including d'Anjou. The guards drove them up the path and the young guard in the gatehouse locked the gate. Bourne ran out of the shadows of the fence into the shadows of the truck. He pulled out his hunting knife and pushed it into the truck's left front tire. He cut the remaining tires of the truck, then moved from car to car, doing the same, until he reached the Russian Zia, only ten meters from the gatehouse.

Silently Bourne opened the door of the Russian car, reached inside, and let off the hand brake. Closing the door as quietly as he had opened it, he put his hands on the back window and pressed his whole weight forward. As the car began to roll toward the fence, he moved around the front of the car next to the Zia and reached into his right back pocket.

Hearing the crash, the surprised guard ran around the gatehouse and into the parking lot, moving his eyes in all directions, then staring at the Zia. He walked to the car door.

Bourne jumped out of the darkness, the handles in both hands, the wire passing over the guard's head. It was done in less than three seconds. The guard was dead.

Removing the radio from the man's belt, Bourne searched the clothes. The man had a gun, the same type as the one he had taken from the dead soldier in Mao's tomb. Instead of one bullet, he now had nine. There was also a wallet with money in it and a document that said he was a member of the People's Republic Intelligence Service. Bourne rolled the body under the car and cut the tires. The big car settled into the ground.

Bourne ran into the gatehouse and, kneeling below the window, removed the bullets from the guard's gun, putting them into his own. He looked around and saw a heavy piece of chain with a lock. There was a ring of keys hanging on the wall. He tried several until the lock opened. He gathered up the chain, went outside, and used it to fix the two gates together. Then he turned and started down the path, staying in the shadows.

He followed it across fields and finally down into a valley. He stopped. Below, about thirty meters ahead, he saw the light of a cigarette. Bourne moved forward silently. He studied the darkness beyond, where lights could be seen now and then through the thick woods of the valley. Flashlights.

Bourne moved into the thick bushes on the right side of the path and began a journey that took twenty minutes before he was close to the guard.

He put away the hunting knife and again reached into his right back pocket for the wire.

He's a human being! A son, a brother, a father!

But he is the enemy! Marie is yours, not theirs.

Bourne jumped out of the grass as the guard lit a cigarette. The smoke exploded from the man's open mouth. His throat was sliced and he fell down, dead.

Pulling out his bloody wire, Bourne shook it in the grass, then rolled the handles together and pushed them back into his pocket. He pulled the body deeper into the bushes and checked its pockets. There was a roll of Chinese paper money, more than several years' income for most Chinese. There were photographs of children, which Bourne put back, and an official document saying that this man was also a member of the People's Republic Intelligence Service! Bourne pulled out the paper he had taken from the first guard's wallet and placed both side by side on the ground. They were the same. He folded them both and put them in his pocket. So simple guards were members of the government's secret police. This operation went to the highest levels of government in Beijing. *No time. It's no concern of yours! Move!*

Bourne took out the bullets from the gun on the man's belt, put them in his pocket, and threw the gun into the bushes. He moved out to the path and started slowly, silently, down toward the lights beyond the wall of high trees below. Some time later, he found himself at the top of a steep valley, looking down through the trees at the gathering below. A circle of flashlights lit up the meeting ground. David Webb felt sick.

Hanging from the branch of a tree by ropes tied to his wrists, his arms stretched out above him, his feet off the ground, a male prisoner twisted in fear, his eyes wide above his gagged mouth.

A thin, middle-aged man dressed in a Mao jacket and pants stood in front of the violently twisting body. His right hand was holding the jeweled handle of an old sword.

"*Listen to me!*" he shouted, as he turned to address his audience. "The nights of the great blade *begin*! And they will continue *night* after *night* until those that have spoken against us are sent to *hell!*" The speaker turned to the tied prisoner. "*You!* Tell the truth and only the truth. Do you know the Westerner?"

The prisoner shook his head wildly.

"Liar!" shouted a voice from the crowd. "He was at Tiananmen Square this afternoon!"

Again the prisoner shook his head in fear.

"He spoke against the true China!" shouted another. "I heard him in the Hua Gong Park among the young people!"

"He opposed our leaders," said the thin man, his voice calm but rising. "When he did this, he disrespected them, and for that the gift of life must be taken away."

The tied man twisted more and more, his cries growing louder, matching the sounds of the other prisoners, who were forced to kneel in front of the speaker. The thin man raised his sword and swung it down and across the stomach of the screaming, twisting body. He then swung it back, cutting through the prisoner's neck. The head fell to the ground in a shower of blood.

As Bourne moved silently to his right, down through the woods toward the tree where the assassin stood watching, a woman was killed in the same way as the man. Another woman, a younger one, was spared. Two brothers, accused of taking money from the group's drug-smuggling operations, were forced to fight each other with knives until one died. The other was allowed to live.

The leader turned to the Frenchman. "Untie his hands," he said. "He's not going anywhere. And remove the gag. We need information from him. Show him we can be trusted."

D'Anjou shook his hands at his sides, then raised his right hand and rubbed his mouth. "Your trust is as believable as your treatment of prisoners," he said in English.

"I forgot," the leader said. "You understand us, don't you?"

"More than you think," replied d'Anjou.

"Good. I prefer speaking English. This is between us, I think."

"There's nothing between us. I try never to deal with madmen."

"You can live," said the leader. "Where is the killer you brought from Macao? Where do you meet?"

"There are no plans to meet."

The man raised his sword. "You tell us or you die—"

"I'll tell you this, Sheng Chouyang. If he could hear my voice, I would explain to him that *you* are the one he must kill. *You* are the man who will bring all Asia to its knees, with millions dying. I would tell him it's *time!*"

Bourne heard him. D'Anjou was sending him a final signal, accepting his own death. Bourne reached into his left front pocket and pulled out the Chinese firecrackers. He moved quickly through the woods until he found a large rock rising several meters out of the ground, large enough to hide his work. He took out the firecrackers and lit the end of the string. The first few centimeters would burn slowly. He quickly went deeper into the woods, unrolling the firecrackers. He reached the end and started back toward the tree.

"What guarantee do I have for my life?" said d'Anjou, almost enjoying himself, planning his own death.

"The truth," replied Sheng. "It's all you need."

Three meters behind the tree, Bourne looked at his watch, concentrating on the second hand. The time for the firecrackers to explode was now. Closing his eyes, he picked up a handful of earth and threw it high to the right of the tree. When he heard the first drops of the shower, d'Anjou threw himself at Sheng Chouyang, striking at his face. Sheng jumped back, swinging the sword at the Frenchman's head. Thankfully, it ended quickly for d'Anjou.

It began! The banging of the firecrackers filled the valley, growing louder as men threw themselves to the ground, shouting in fear, frightened for their lives.

The impostor moved behind a tree trunk, his weapon in his hand. Bourne, with the silencer fixed to his gun, walked up and stood over him. He took aim and fired, blowing the weapon out of the assassin's hand. The killer spun around, his eyes wide. Bourne fired again, just to the side of his head.

"Turn around!" ordered Bourne, pushing the gun into the assassin's left eye. "Now hold the tree! Both arms—tighter!"

Bourne pushed the weapon into the back of the killer's neck as he looked around the trunk. The leader was rising from the ground, shouting orders, and demanding a weapon. Bourne stepped away from the tree and raised his gun. Their eyes met. Bourne fired just as Sheng pulled a guard in front of him. The soldier bent back, his neck breaking as the bullets hit him. Sheng held on to the body, using it for protection, as Bourne fired twice more, hitting the guard's dead body. He could not hit Sheng! He could not do what d'Anjou had told him to do! *I'm sorry, d'Anjou! No time! Move! D'Anjou is gone … Marie!*

The assassin moved his head, trying to see. Bourne fired his gun. Wood exploded in the impostor's face as he put his hands up to his eyes, then shook his head, trying to see clearly again.

"Move!" ordered Bourne, holding the assassin's throat and turning him around. "You're coming with me!"

Chapter 13   Out of China

Alexander Conklin walked into the office of the house on Victoria Peak. Havilland rose from the chair and came around the desk, his hand held out. McAllister stayed seated.

"Mr. Conklin?"

"Keep your hand, Mr. Ambassador. I don't want to get infected."

"I see. Anger means you can't be polite."

"No, I really don't want to catch anything. As they say over here, you're bad luck. You're carrying some disease, I think."

"And what might that be?"

"Death."

"Please, Mr. Conklin, you can do better than that."

"No, I mean it. Less than twenty minutes ago I saw somebody killed, cut down in the street with forty or fifty bullets in her."

"Webb's wife is dead?" shouted McAllister.

"No, but thanks for telling me you're worried about her."

"Good God!" cried the ambassador. "It was Catherine Staples!"

"Give the man a prize. Nice to know that you were worried about her, too. Are you planning to have dinner with the Canadian consul soon? I'd love to be there."

"Shut up, you fool!' shouted Havilland, crossing over and falling into his chair. He leaned back, his eyes closed.

"That's the one thing I'm not going to do," said Conklin, stepping forward. "You are *responsible* ... *sir*!" The CIA man leaned over the edge of the desk. "Just as you're responsible for what's happened to David and Marie Webb! Who the *hell* do you think you are?" Conklin sat down, his back straight, his wooden foot bent to one side. "Talk to me," he said. "I want to hear your story."

"First the woman. Webb's wife. She's all right? She's safe?"

"No, she's not all right. Her husband's missing and she doesn't know whether he's alive or dead. But she's safe. With me."

"We're *desperate*," begged the diplomat. "We need her!"

"You've also got a spy in this house. Somebody arranged for Catherine Staples to die because of what she learned here. I won't put Marie in that sort of danger."

"Conklin, *listen* to me! If there's a spy, we'll find him, but this is more important. I know that Webb's in Beijing. If somehow he comes out with the assassin and his wife isn't in place, he'll kill the only connection we *must have*! Without it, we're all lost."

"So that was the plan from the beginning. Jason Bourne hunts Jason Bourne."

"Yes, but without the complications there was no chance of him agreeing. We wouldn't have our hunter."

"You really *are* garbage," said Conklin slowly. He settled into the chair. "Start at the beginning. I want to hear it step by step."

"All right. I'll begin with a name that I'm sure you recognize. Sheng Chouyang."

♦

Dawn. Wetness everywhere. The single runway beyond the fence ran black across the short grass of the small airport. Bourne's car was far off the road, hidden by bushes. The impostor, tied with wire by his thumbs and wrists, could not move.

Bourne reached for the roll of clothing he had removed from his back. There was a large Mao jacket, a pair of wide pants, and a cloth hat that was standard. He put on the hat and jacket, then pulled the pants over his own and turned to the assassin.

"Move toward the fence," he said, bending down and digging

into his bag. "Get on your knees and lean into it," he continued, pulling out a two-meter length of thin rope. "Press your face against it. Eyes to the front! Hurry *up*!"

The killer did as he was told. Bourne walked over and pushed the rope through the fence on the right side of the assassin's neck, then reached through and pulled the line across his face and back through. He pulled it tight and tied it around the assassin's neck.

"What the hell are you—*oh, God*!"

Bourne took the wire cutter from the bag and cut the wires right around the assassin's body. He stepped back and raised his right foot, placing it between the assassin's shoulders. He pushed his leg forward. Killer and fence fell onto the grass on the other side.

"Oh God!" cried the assassin in pain. "Very funny, aren't you?"

"Get up and keep your voice down."

Slowly, the assassin got to his feet. Bourne reached over and pulled the knot free, holding on to one end of the line. The fence fell away, and before the assassin could move, Bourne pulled the rope around the assassin's head so that it was caught in his mouth. He pulled it tight, stretching the assassin's jaw open.

"I can't take credit for this," said Bourne. "I watched d'Anjou and the others die. You saw them, too, and you smiled. How does it feel? ... Oh, I forgot, you can't answer, can you?"

He pushed the assassin forward toward the shadow of a building.

Suddenly, powerful lights lit up the field and yellow lights appeared along the whole length of the runway. Men ran out of the buildings. The lights of the main building were turned on.

Bourne looked up and saw the plane, lights flashing on its wings, come down out of the sky and land.

"*Get that fuel truck to the plane!*" shouted a voice in Chinese, the man pointing to one of three trucks to the side of the runway.

A group of officials got out of the plane while the fuel truck drove across to it. With the assassin in front, Bourne's gun pointing past his head, the two men ran across to the other fuel trucks. Bourne ordered the assassin to kneel down in front of him as he opened his bag and took out a roll of bandage. Then he removed the hunting knife from his belt and pulled a hosepipe off the truck, dropping it to the ground. He pushed his knife into the hosepipe where it entered the truck and made a cut, enough for a small stream of gasoline to run out. He rose to his feet and pointed his gun at the assassin while he handed him the roll of bandage.

"Pull out about two meters and wet it with the fuel there." The killer knelt down and followed Bourne's instructions. "Now," continued Bourne, "push the end of the bandage into the hole where I've cut the hosepipe. Further—further. Use your thumb."

Bourne looked quickly over at the refueling—no, refueled airplane. Men were climbing off the wings and putting the hosepipes back into the fuel truck. The pilot and flight officer were walking around the plane, making their final check. They would get back into the plane in less than a minute. Bourne reached into his pocket for matches and threw them down in front of the assassin. "Light it. *Now*!"

"It'll go up like a bomb! It'll blow us both into the sky!"

"No. Lay the bandage on the wet grass—"

"Slowing down the fire—?"

"Hurry up! *Do* it!"

"*Done*!"

The flames jumped up from the end of the bandage, then fell back and began to move slowly along it.

"Get in front of me," ordered Bourne. "Start walking."

The fuel truck began backing away from the plane, then circled around to take up its position next to the truck with the lighted bandage heading into its fuel supply. Bourne turned his head. The bandage had burst into its final flame.

The pilot waved to his flight officer. They marched toward the door of the plane.

"Be ready to run!" shouted Bourne.

They turned right toward the plane. It happened. The fuel truck exploded, sending fire into the sky as pieces of metal blew above and to the sides of the burning vehicle. The truck crews screamed and raced in all directions.

"*Run!*" shouted Bourne.

Both men raced to the plane and the door, where the pilot was looking out in shock while the flight officer remained frozen on the ladder.

"Move!" shouted Bourne in Chinese, keeping his face in the shadows. "*Get this plane out of here!*"

A second truck blew up, turning the area into an ocean of fire.

"You're right!" shouted the pilot, pulling the flight officer inside. Both raced forward to the controls.

It is the moment, thought Bourne. "Get in!" he ordered the assassin as the third fuel truck blew up.

"*Right!*" shouted the assassin. Then suddenly, he spun around on the ladder, his right foot swinging toward Bourne.

Bourne was ready. He crashed the gun into the assassin's ankle, then swung it up, hitting the assassin's forehead. Blood ran as the killer fell back into the plane. Bourne jumped up the steps, kicking the unconscious body of the impostor back across the metal floor. He pulled the door shut. The airplane began to move forward. Bourne pulled a second length of rope from his bag and tied the assassin's wrists to the legs of two seats.

He got up and started forward. The plane was now on the runway but suddenly the engines were cut. The plane stopped in front of the main building, where a group of government officials were gathered, watching the fires burning toward the north.

"Hello," said Bourne, placing his gun against the back of the pilot's head. The second pilot turned around in his seat. "Take off!" he said. "Fly south! And give me your maps."

Chapter 14 The House on Victoria Peak

Conklin entered Havilland's office and sat down without saying a word.

"Good afternoon," Havilland said. The ambassador looked pale and tired. "Bourne's in Hong Kong, with the assassin."

"That's good," said Conklin.

"Yes, but there's a problem. The deal was that when he called, he had to hear Marie's voice within thirty seconds or he'd kill the assassin. That wasn't possible because we didn't have Marie."

"Don't expect me to feel bad about it," said Conklin.

Havilland ran his hand through his gray hair. "We put our own telephone operator on the line. She said there was a problem with the connection and kept him talking long enough for us to work out which hotel he was staying in. Then we sent some people around to bring him in. We planned to hold Bourne until you brought Marie here."

"You *planned* to … You mean it went wrong?"

"Yes."

"Not surprising. He isn't stupid. Hong Kong telephone operators don't keep people talking. So what happened?"

"Two of the men who got to the hotel were found tied up and badly injured. He made one of them talk. Now he knows that Marie was sick and escaped. Quite possibly he thinks she's dead now. He knows there's no taipan, that *we're* running this operation, and he knows where this house is."

Conklin stood up. "I'll go and get Marie. One thing you can be sure of: Bourne is coming here, and he's coming here to kill

70

you. I don't think you can stop him, but maybe *she* can."

◆

Bourne drove the old car off the side of the road. There was no need to hide it; he would not be coming back. He did not want to come back. Marie was gone and it was finished.

He climbed out of the car and opened the back door. The assassin was in the back seat, his hands and legs tied and with a piece of cloth tied around his mouth. Bourne cut the ropes but left the cloth in place. With his gun against the back of the assassin's neck, they walked up the road to the house on Victoria Peak.

By the gate, Bourne reached into his pocket and pulled out a small package of plastic explosive. He pressed the sticky side against the wall. He had already set the timer for seven minutes. "*Move!*" he whispered.

They went around the corner of the wall and walked along it to a place where the branches of a tree hung over it. "Here!" Bourne whispered. He removed the wire cutters from his bag and pushed the assassin against the wall. Then he stepped back and bent his right leg in front of the killer as he handed him the wire cutters. "Stand on my leg, reach up, and cut the wires." The prisoner did as he was told. "Climb up there," said Bourne.

The killer did so and as his left leg swung over the wall, Bourne jumped up to take hold of the assassin's pants and pulled himself up against the stone, swinging his own left leg over the top. The two men faced each other on the wall.

"Nicely done," Bourne said. "Not much longer now."

An explosion filled the night sky as the gate blew up. Bourne reached into his bag, removing a tear gas grenade. Thirty meters away there was a large window. He threw the grenade through the glass. Inside the house he could see running figures, then the lights were turned off, but blinding white lights came on outside.

"Jump!" whispered Bourne, swinging his leg off the wall and

knocking the assassin to the ground. He followed while the assassin was still falling, and took hold of his shoulder while he was still kneeling on the grass. Bourne pulled the cloth from the impostor's mouth. "I'm giving you a chance." He handed the man a gun. "Mine's on *you*, and don't you forget it. In a few minutes you can run for the wall, or the gate, anywhere you like. You'll lead them away from me."

The assassin took hold of the weapon as gunfire hit leaves and branches all along the wall. Soldiers attacked, running beside the stone, rifles ready to fire. Bourne pulled a second plastic explosive packet from his bag, set the timer for ten seconds and threw it as far as he could toward the back garden wall, away from the guard.

"Come on!" he ordered the assassin, pushing his gun into the killer's back. "You in front. Down this path. Nearer the house."

The explosion came about forty meters away at the back of the grounds. Trees and dirt, bushes and whole beds of flowers flamed into the air. "Move!" whispered Bourne.

He closed his eyes in anger as rifle fire filled the back garden. *They were children. They fired blindly out of fear.*

Another group of soldiers, obviously led by an experienced officer, took up positions in front of the great house and circled it. Bourne again reached into his bag, and removed one of two fire bombs he had bought in Mongkok. He pulled off the cover. Underneath, the surface was sticky and would hold onto anything. The sides of the house were made of wood, above a lower stone border. He threw the bomb at the wood, far above and to the left of a pair of glass doors. It stuck there and the wall of the house blew apart. The flames spread quickly, running along the wood and inside the house.

Bourne removed another plastic explosive charge, set the timer, and threw it over the bushes. "Go through there!" he ordered, pushing the assassin into the row of bushes. Bourne ran after him, hitting him on the head with the gun, stopping him. "Just a few more minutes, then you're on your own."

The fourth explosion took away two meters of the side wall. Perhaps because they expected enemy soldiers to pour through, the soldier guards opened fire on the fallen stones. Bourne pulled out his next to last plastic packet, set the timer for ninety seconds, and threw it toward the corner of the back wall, where the grounds were empty. He took out the tear gas grenade and spoke to the assassin. "Turn around." The assassin did so, Bourne's gun in front of his eyes. "Take this," said Bourne. "When I tell you, throw it into the stone to the right of the glass doors. The gas will spread, blinding most of those kids. They won't be able to shoot so don't waste bullets. You haven't got many."

The killer did not at first reply. Instead he raised his weapon level with Bourne's and aimed it at his head. "Now, which of us has the most to lose?" he said. "I can take a bullet in the head. I've been waiting for it for years. But I don't think you can accept the idea of not getting inside that house." There was a sudden sound of voices and another burst of gunfire as soldiers rushed to the broken side wall. "Empty your bag of tricks, Webb."

"There's nothing left."

"Let's see," said the assassin, his left hand slowly reaching out, softly touching the bag on Bourne's right side, their eyes locked. The killer felt the cloth, squeezing it in several places. Slowly, he moved his hand back. "You lied. There's a machine gun in there. That gun could get me out of here. *Give!* Or one of us dies right here. Right now."

The plastic explosive blew up and shook the ground; the surprised assassin's eyes moved to the side, just for a second. It was enough. Bourne's hand moved up, pushing the killer's gun away, crashing his heavy gun into the side of the assassin's head with the force of a hammer. The assassin fell to his left. Bourne put a knee on his wrist and pulled his gun free.

"You keep begging for a quick death," said Bourne, as the noise reached its height in the gardens. "You really don't like yourself, do you? But you had a good idea. I *will* empty my bag of tricks. It's almost time now."

Bourne emptied his open bag. The contents fell on the grass. There was one fire bomb and one plastic explosive packet left as well as the MAC-10 machine gun. He loaded it. He lifted up the fire bomb, pulled off the covering, and threw it at the wall above the glass doors. It stuck to the wood. Then he threw a tear gas grenade. It exploded, falling to the ground; the smoke spread quickly, making the men near it cough. They rubbed their swollen, watery eyes and covered their noses.

The second fire bomb exploded above the glass doors, breaking the glass into pieces. Flames spread upward toward the roof and inside. The soldiers ran away from the explosion and the flames into the clouds of tear gas. A number of them now dropped their rifles as they tried to find fresh air.

Bourne rose, the machine gun in his hand, pulling the assassin up beside him. It was time. "Thirty seconds." Bourne threw the last plastic explosive packet as far as he could toward the right front wall.

"My *weapon*! Give me the gun!" It was on the ground, under Bourne's foot.

The last explosion blew up a tree, its roots crashing into a weakened section of the wall, stones falling out of place. Soldiers from the gate rushed forward. "Now!" shouted Bourne, rising to his full height.

"Give me the *gun*! Let go of it."

Jason Bourne suddenly froze. He could not move—except that, somehow, he crashed his knee up into the killer's throat, sending the assassin over on his side. A man had appeared beyond the broken glass doors of the burning house. Bourne knew the face. It was his *enemy*. Alexander Conklin had tried to kill him.

"*David*! It's Alex. Don't do what you're *doing*! Stop it! It's *me*, David! I'm here to help you!"

"You're here to *kill* me! You came to kill me in Paris—you tried again in New York! You have a short memory!"

"I know the whole story, David. I flew over here to help. Marie, Mo Panov, and I—we're all here. Marie's safe!"

"More *lies*!" Bourne fired his machine gun. Bullets went everywhere, but for reasons unknown to Bourne, they did not cut down Conklin. "I'm going inside! I want the silent, secret man behind you! They're *there*! I know they're there!"

Bourne took hold of the fallen assassin and pulled him to his feet, handing him the gun. "You wanted a Jason Bourne—he's *yours*! I'm letting him go. Kill him while I kill *you*!"

The assassin ran through the bushes away from Bourne. There was a burst of rifle fire. The assassin dove to the ground, rolling over and over to avoid the bullets.

"Stop it! Not *him*! Don't *kill* him!" screamed Conklin.

Bourne swung around and aimed his weapon at the soldiers moving toward him. He fired several bursts, moving from place to place behind the roses. *But he aimed above their heads. Why? Because it was not right that soldiers should die for the men inside the house.*

"*David*!" A woman's voice. "David, David, *David*!" A woman ran out of the house. She took hold of Alexander Conklin and pushed him away. She stood alone. "It's *me*, David! I'm *here*! I'm *safe*! Everything's all *right*, my darling!"

An old woman with gray hair. Another trick, another lie.

"Get out of my way, lady, or I'll kill you. You're just another lie, another *trick*!"

Suddenly the assassin was on his feet, moving toward the soldier nearest him, who was still coughing from the gas. The killer took the soldier's rifle and shot him. The man fell forward holding his stomach. The assassin turned and ran for the wall, firing his rifle as he went.

"You killed my friend!" It was the cry of a very young man. "You're going to die!"

A black soldier jumped away from his dead white friend and raced toward the wall as the assassin began to climb the broken stones. The soldier fired again and again.

A scream—the scream of death.

Bourne started forward, his weapon raised. Marie ran toward him, the distance between them no more than meters.

"Don't *do* it, David!"

"I'm not David, lady! Ask your nasty friend—we have a long shared history. Get out of my way!" *Why couldn't he kill her?*

"All right!" screamed Marie, not moving. "There's no David, *all right*? You're Jason Bourne! You're anything you want to be, but you're also *mine*! You're my *husband*!"

The news hit the guards like lightning. The officers held up their hands to their men as they all stared in surprise.

"I don't *know* you!"

"My voice is my own. You know it, Jason."

"A *trick*! She's an *actress*! A *lie*! It's been done before."

"And if I look different, it's because of you, *Jason Bourne*!"

"Get out of my way or get *killed*!"

"You taught me in *Paris*! You taught me how to change my appearance, my hair. That's all I've *done*, Jason!"

"*No*!" cried Bourne, lengthening the word into a scream.

"All right, Jason. If you don't know me, I don't want to live. I can't be clearer than that, my darling."

Bourne raised the machine gun, aiming at the gray hair. His finger tightened. Suddenly, his right hand began to shake, then his left. Then the shaking spread to his head. It moved from side to side as his neck began to lose control.

Jason Bourne dropped the weapon and David Webb fell to his knees, crying. Marie started toward him.

"No!" commanded a new voice—Morris Panov's. "He has to come to you. He has to recognise you."

Silence. Lights. Fire.

David Webb raised his head, the tears running down his face. Slowly he rose to his feet and ran into the arms of his wife.

♦

The photograph was taken on the white conference table by an embassy photographer. A bloody white sheet covered Webb's body; it was pulled down to his throat, showing a blood-covered face, the eyes wide open.

"Develop the roll as fast as you can and bring me the prints," instructed Conklin.

"Twenty minutes," said the photographer, heading for the door, as McAllister entered the room.

"So what's happening?" asked Webb, sitting up on the table, as Marie wiped his face with a warm, wet towel.

"The consulate press officers said they'd give the reporters some news in an hour or so, as soon as all the facts were in place. The full story, with the photograph, will be in the morning papers. After that the public will think that you're the man who died on Victoria Peak."

"I have to get out of here," Bourne said. "I have to get to Macao as quickly as possible."

"David, please!" Marie stood in front of her husband, staring at him, her voice low and strong.

"I don't want it to be this way," said Webb, getting off the table, "but I have to start the process of contacting Sheng before the story appears in the papers. He has to believe *I'm* his assassin, not the Jason Bourne who tried to kill him in that forest. He has to get word from me—from who he thinks I am—before he's given any other information. Because I'm sending him the last thing he wants to hear."

"What are you going to tell him?" asked the ambassador, his voice showing that he disliked losing control of this operation.

"What you told me. Part truth, part lie."

"Tell us, Mr. Webb," said Havilland firmly. "We owe you a great deal but—"

"You *owe* me what you can't *pay* me!" shouted Jason Bourne. "Unless you blow your brains out right here and now."

"I understand your anger, but I must know that you will not put at risk the lives of the people of Hong Kong or the interests of the United States. "

"Very well," Webb said. "I'll tell you. A spoken message is sent to Sheng. It contains enough of the truth to alarm him. Let's say that the sender of the message is somebody in Hong Kong who will lose millions if Sheng's plan falls apart. The message could mention spies, information that has become public, people changing sides, criminals getting together because they've been cut out—all the things that you're certain will happen. Sheng will have to act—he can't afford not to. Contacts will be made and a meeting arranged. The man in Hong Kong will be as anxious to protect himself as Sheng, and as nervous, demanding a safe meeting ground. That's the trap."

"Very quick and very professional," said the ambassador. "And with a problem. Where do we find this person in Hong Kong?"

Jason Bourne looked at Havilland coldly. "You make him up," he said. Then he turned to McAllister and said, "Now, I need you to get me into Macao—quietly."

Chapter 15 Sheng Chouyang

The Emergency Medical Service helicopter flew across Victoria Harbour toward Macao. The gunboats of the People's Republic of China had been told not to fire at it. McAllister had been lucky: a visiting party official from Beijing had been admitted to the Kiang Wu Hospital, seriously sick. He needed a rare type of blood, which was always in short supply.

Bourne and the undersecretary wore white coats. The hospital's parking area had been cleared of vehicles and four searchlights lit it up. The pilot began to lose height.

Despite his dislike of the undersecretary, Bourne had to admire McAllister's ability to organize. He had demanded the repayment of an old debt tonight, from a doctor at the Kiang Wu Hospital who several years ago had stolen American medical money. McAllister had found out but did not have him fired because there was a shortage of doctors, and since then the man had known that he owed him.

"Come on!" shouted Bourne, rising and picking up one of the two bottles of blood. "Move!"

Minutes later, now dressed in dark pants and loose-fitting jackets, Bourne and McAllister watched the helicopter rise up from the landing area and disappear into the night sky. Inside, dressed in white coats, were the two young Portuguese doctors who had taken their place, looking forward to a night in Hong Kong.

"Let's go," said Bourne. The two men started to walk. "Why are you here?" he asked.

"What do you mean?"

"You got me to Macao. I don't need you now. I can get to Sheng."

"All right, I'll say it now. As the assassin, you're the connection with Sheng, but I'm the one that can bring him to you."

"You?"

"It was the reason I told the embassy to give my name to reporters. Sheng knows me. I don't think your idea will work. Sheng won't accept a conference with an unknown person, but he will with somebody he knows."

"Havilland thought it would work."

"No he didn't. He thought it might, possibly. What does he have to lose? If you die, it doesn't cost him anything."

"Why would Sheng accept a meeting with you?"

"Because he knows I have done many things for my government, but I haven't risen to the top level, or to a well-paid job for a private company. I'm a failure, like Alexander Conklin. So now I want to be part of Sheng's plans for Hong Kong. I was nearly killed last night and now I want something for myself, for my family. That's the lie."

"But what do you have to offer him?"

"You're not thinking. I was sent out here to check if this story about Sheng's plans for Hong Kong was true. It is, of course, and all the details are written in a file. It's in a safe in the house on Victoria Peak. For a price, I can destroy that file and write a report saying that Sheng is innocent. But he'd have to meet with me to arrange this."

"Then what?"

"Then you tell me what to do, how to kill him."

"You'll get killed."

"I'll accept the risk."

"Why?"

"Because it has to be done. Havilland's right about that. And the moment Sheng's guards see that you're not the impostor, that you're the original assassin, they will kill you."

"I never planned for him to see me," said Bourne quietly. "You were going to take care of that, but not this way."

In the dark street, McAllister stopped and stared at Bourne. "You're taking me with you, aren't you?" he said finally.

"Yes."

"I thought you would. I even brought my diplomatic passport." McAllister paused for a second. "And one for you."

"I have three false passports with me," Bourne said.

"These are better. They'll get us into China without visas. I expect you know somebody here who can change a photograph."

Bourne nodded. "Why didn't you tell Havilland about this grand plan of yours?" he asked.

"Because he wouldn't have allowed it. He doesn't think I'm good enough to make it work. And that's one reason I'm doing it—I'm rather tired of people seeing me as very intelligent but ineffective. I want my big moment."

They started walking again, through more dark streets. "Have you considered what will happen if you fail? You're a United States undersecretary of state. Very embarrassing."

"The government's protected. It's all written down in my papers back at Victoria Peak, with a set for Havilland and another to be delivered to the Chinese consulate in Hong Kong within three days if I don't return. So I can't turn back now."

"What the hell have you *done!*"

"Described a serious disagreement between Sheng and myself, because he cut me out of his Hong Kong operation. I spent years out here, so it's quite believable. Certainly, Sheng's enemies in the government will be happy. If I'm killed, they'll have so many questions for him that he won't dare act—if he lives."

"My God," said Bourne, shocked.

"Now, how do we reach Beijing?

With his eyes closed, Bourne answered, "A soldier in Guangdong named Soo Jiang. I speak to him in French and he leaves a message for us here in Macao. At a table in a casino."

"Good," said McAllister. "But first I need a weapon."

This was not a great problem. D'Anjou's apartment was not far away and it held a collection of guns. They simply had to get inside and choose those most easily taken to pieces so they could cross the border at Guangdong with diplomatic passports. But it took more than two hours as Bourne put gun after gun in McAllister's hand, and watched how he held them. The weapon

81

finally chosen was the smallest in d'Anjou's collection, a Charter Arms .22 with a silencer.

"Aim for the head, at least three bullets. Anything else would be a waste of time."

McAllister swallowed, staring at the gun, as Bourne studied the weapons and chose for himself three small Interdynamic KG-9 machine guns that each held thirty bullets.

"Now let's go to the casino and make contact," Bourne said.

♦

They crossed the border in full darkness, now in business suits and ties instead of the old clothes they had worn previously. They carried small cases wrapped in diplomatic tape, which couldn't be opened at borders. These held their weapons as well as several additional things that Bourne had picked up in d'Anjou's apartment after McAllister had produced the important tape that was respected even by the People's Republic of China.

"He's in the air," said Bourne, as they walked along the street. "He's on his way here. We'll be followed. You know that, don't you?"

"No, I don't know that," replied McAllister, looking quickly at Bourne. "Sheng will be cautious. I've given him enough information to worry him. If he thought there was only one file—which is in fact the truth—he might take chances, thinking he could buy it from me and kill me. But he thinks, or has to believe, that there's a copy in Washington. That's the one he wants destroyed. He won't do anything to make me run."

"Maybe not, but he won't fly in here completely unprotected. The soldiers won't be far away."

Not long after that, and like a large bird, the helicopter came down onto a field. McAllister stood in full view and the machine's searchlight found him. Jason Bourne was around forty meters away, in the shadows of the woods. He could be seen, but not clearly. The engines shut down and there was silence. The door opened, the stairs were put in place, and the thin, gray-haired Sheng Chouyang walked down the steps, carrying a briefcase.

"So good to see you after all these years, Edward," he called out. He looked at what he thought was the assassin in the shadows, then moved to his right. "Let's talk quietly together, Edward. This is a private matter."

Bourne raced to the helicopter while the two men were standing with their backs to him. The pilot's door was open.

"Keep quiet," whispered Bourne, showing his KG-9 machine gun. He pulled a piece of cloth tight over the shocked, open mouth. Then, with a long, thin cord, he tied the man to his seat, then tied his arms. There would be no sudden take-off.

Returning the weapon to the belt under his jacket, Bourne left the helicopter and walked rapidly back to his previous position. He wondered what was being said between the two enemies. He wondered what McAllister was waiting for.

"Did you really think that we, the great men of the most ancient and cultured country the world has ever known, would leave it to unwashed farmers believing in out-of-date theories of equality?" Sheng stood in front of McAllister, holding his briefcase across his chest with both hands. "They should be our slaves, not our rulers."

"It was that kind of thinking that lost you the country—you, the Nationalist leaders, not the people. Nobody asked them."

"One does not discuss things with Marxist animals, or with liars—as I will not discuss things with you, Edward." With his left hand Sheng opened his briefcase and pulled out a file. "Do you recognize it?" he asked calmly.

"I don't *believe* it!"

"Believe, my old friend. One of my men stole it last night, from the house on Victoria Peak."

"It's impossible!"

"It's here. In my hand. And the opening page states clearly that there is only one copy, to be sent with soldiers guarding it wherever it goes. Quite correctly, in my judgment. The contents would start a war in the Far East."

"I had a copy made and sent to Washington," said the undersecretary quickly, quietly, firmly.

"I don't believe that," said Sheng. "All diplomatic messages must be seen by the highest officer. Havilland wouldn't allow it."

"I sent a copy to the Chinese consulate!" shouted McAllister. "You're finished, Sheng!"

"Really? Who do you think receives *all* messages coming into our consulate in Hong Kong? Don't bother to answer—I'll do it for you. One of our people." Sheng paused, his eyes suddenly on fire. "We are *everywhere*, Edward! We will have our nation back again! We cannot be *stopped*!"

"You *can* be stopped," said McAllister quietly, his right hand moving to the fold in his jacket. "*I'll* stop you."

Suddenly Sheng dropped his briefcase, showing a gun. He fired as McAllister jumped back in terror, holding his shoulder.

"Dive!" shouted Bourne, racing in front of the airplane and firing his machine gun. "Roll, *roll*! If you can move, roll *away*!"

"You!" Sheng screamed, firing two quick shots down into the fallen undersecretary of state, then raising his weapon and repeatedly firing, aiming at the man running toward him.

"For d'Anjou!" shouted Bourne. "For all the people that you cut to death!"

A short burst exploded from the machine gun—then no *more*. It was *stuck*! Sheng knew it; he leveled his weapon carefully as Bourne threw the gun down, running toward the killer. Sheng fired; Bourne spun to his right as he pulled his knife from his belt, then changed direction and struck at Sheng. The knife found its mark and Bourne cut open Sheng's chest. The actual killer of hundreds and the would-be killer of millions was dead.

Bourne looked downhill. Six soldiers were running toward them, across a neighboring field. He bent over the body of McAllister, who was moving both arms, his right hand stretched out, desperately trying to reach something.

"Mac, can you *hear* me?"

"The file!" whispered the undersecretary of State. "Get the *file!*"

"What—?" Bourne looked over at the body of Sheng Chouyang and saw the black-bordered file, one of the most secret, most explosive documents on Earth. He reached for it. "Listen to me, Mac! I have to move you, and it may hurt, but we have no choice. Soldiers are on their way here."

Bourne carried McAllister toward the helicopter. Suddenly he cried out, "God, *wait* a minute! I have to go back."

He leaned McAllister against the side of the machine and raced back to the body of Sheng Chouyang. When he reached it, he bent down and pushed a flat object under the dead man's jacket. He rose and ran back to the helicopter, then carefully, gently, helped McAllister to lie down across two of the back seats. Bourne jumped in the front, took out his knife and cut the cord that tied the pilot, then the cloth that gagged him.

"Get into the air," Bourne shouted. "Now!"

The pilot moved the switches and started the engine as the soldiers got closer. One of them reached Sheng's body, looked at it, then fired at the slowly rising helicopter. The others joined in. Bullets began to strike the machine.

"Get out of here!" shouted Bourne.

"This is Sheng's machine. The metal is thick and no bullet can break the glass," said the pilot calmly. "Where do we go?"

"Hong Kong!" shouted Bourne, surprised to see that the pilot turned to him, smiling.

"Surely the generous Americans or British will welcome me, sir? It is a dream come true."

"Mr. Webb," whispered McAllister from the back seat.

Webb turned around. "What is it? How are you feeling?"

"Never mind that. Why did you go back—back to Sheng?"

"To give him a goodbye present. A bankbook. It shows a large amount of money in his name in the Cayman Islands."

"*What?*"

"It won't do anybody any good. The names and numbers have been cut out. But it will be interesting to see how Beijing reacts, won't it?"

♦

The sun slowly disappeared into the Pacific Ocean, letting night fall on Hawaii. They walked along the beach, holding hands, their bodies touching—so natural, so right.

"What do you do when there's a part of you that you hate?" asked David Webb.

"Accept it," answered Marie. "We all have a dark side, David. We want to deny it, but we can't. It's there. Maybe we can't exist without it. Yours is a story called Jason Bourne, but that's all it is."

"I hate him."

"He brought you back to me. That's all that matters."

ACTIVITIES

Chapter 1

Before you read

1 Read the Introduction. Match these dates to the events below.

   1842   1860   1898   1949   the 1980s   1997

   a The start of the People's Republic of China.

   b Hong Kong became part of China again.

   c Discussions about the future of Hong Kong.

   d Britain obtained land near Hong Kong Island.

   e Hong Kong Island became a British colony.

   f An agreement was signed between Britain and China.

2 Look at the map on page vii. Find these places.

   a a hill on Hong Kong Island

   b a city to the west of Kowloon

   c a village on the border with China

   d an airport in Kowloon

   e a university

3 Look at the Word List at the back of the book. Read the definitions of words that are new to you. Then find words for:

   a two things that can explode.

   b two jobs in which a person is an assistant.

   c three places where people work outside their own country.

While you read

4 Decide whether these sentences are true (T) or false (F).

   a The nightclub is on Hong Kong Island.   .....

   b The manager treats the priest with respect.   .....

   c A man in the nightclub is working for the priest.   .....

   d The priest shoots the guard.   .....

   e The priest writes a name in blood.   .....

   f The priest leaves a machine gun in his robe.   .....

   g The priest has killed an important politician.   .....

   h The manager believes that the assassin is
   Jason Bourne.   .....

87

After you read

5 Discuss these questions.

    a Why might the Vice-Premier of the People's Republic of China be in a nightclub in Hong Kong?

    b Why does the manager say, "Hong Kong is dead."?

    c Why does the killer leave a cloth with a name on it?

    d Who is the killer working for?

Chapters 2–3

Before you read

6 Which of these do you think will happen in this part of the book? Why?

    a There will be war between the People's Republic of China and Hong Kong.

    b The Americans will send somebody to capture the "priest".

    c The British will tell the Americans to stay out of Hong Kong.

    d The "priest" will be killed.

While you read

7 Three men have used the name Jason Bourne. Write a number, 1, 2 or 3 (for the 1st, 2nd, and 3rd Bourne), after each of these sentences.

    a He has worked for a Chinese politician. .....

    b He was shot in the head and died. .....

    c He was shot in the head but didn't die. .....

    d He worked for the U.S. government. .....

    e He worked for the enemy. .....

    f He killed the Vice-Premier in Kowloon. .....

    g The U.S. government tried to kill him. .....

After you read

8 McAllister says, "I can't believe what I've done." Webb didn't kill anyone in Kowloon. Marie has been kidnapped. What does all of this mean? What is happening here? Discuss your ideas with another student.

9 Use a library or the Internet to find about more about the work of an ambassador, an embassy, and the State Department of the United States government.

Chapters 4–5

Before you read

10 When Bourne flies into Hong Kong, he knows one important fact: somebody has arranged a suite for him at the Regent Hotel in Kowloon. How will he find out who did this? Discuss your ideas with another student.

While you read

11 *Do the unexpected. Confuse the enemy. Jason Bourne.*

In these chapters, Webb does a number of things to confuse the enemy. Number them in the correct order from 1 to 8.

a	He pays a woman for information.	.....
b	He arrives early for an appointment.	.....
c	He changes his room in the hotel.	.....
d	He sticks an ice pick into a wall.	.....
e	He follows the assistant manager of the hotel.	.....
f	He attacks three men.	.....
g	He stops all calls to his phone.	.....
h	He discovers a telephone number.	.....

After you read

12 "I'll be asking you to pay for the suit," he said. "White isn't my color." Who says these words? Why is the suit important? What does it tell us?

13 Which of these places does David Webb visit in Chapters 4 and 5? Use the map on page vii to help you.

a	Aberdeen	**f**	Repulse Bay
b	Central District	**g**	Tuen Mun
c	Kai Tak Airport	**h**	Victoria Peak
d	Kowloon Walled City	**i**	Wanchai
e	Mongkok		

Chapters 6–7

Before you read

14 When she spoke to David in Hong Kong, Marie said, "That lovely street with the row of green trees, my favorite tree—" Marie was trying to tell him something. In Chapter 7 McAllister works it out—she wants to meet David at the Canadian consulate. What is the connection? Discuss your ideas with another student.

While you read

15 Webb gets some pieces of information about the assassin. Number them in the order he hears them, from 1 to 8.

a He is an Englishman. .....
b He works from Macao. .....
c His contact is a man who fights very well. .....
d He looks like David Webb. .....
e He works for a Chinese politician. .....
f He is on the run from the British police. .....
g Contact is made at the Kam Pek casino. .....
h He works with a Frenchman. .....

After you read

16 *That's the big Chinese man. He's been nice to me. These are not bad people. This is a government operation.* Marie has this thought when she is in hospital. So do you think she was right to escape? Would it not be better to wait and see what happens? Discuss your ideas with another student.

17 Use a library or the Internet to find about more about the work of a consulate and a consul. How is a consulate different from an embassy?

Chapters 8–9

Before you read

18 Which one of these do you think Catherine will do now?

a She will buy an air ticket for Marie and send her home.
b She will hide Marie and try to find out more.
c She will see Havilland and ask for an explanation.
d She will see Havilland and have an argument with him.
e She will give Marie's story to the newspapers.

While you read

19 Who says what? Write the numbers.

1) Ambassador Havilland   **4)** David Webb
2) Catherine Staples   **5)** Edward McAllister
3) d'Anjou   **6)** Marie Webb

a	"You're very tiring."	.....
b	"And, by God, you live with what happens!"	.....
c	"I believe you, Mr. President."	.....
d	"You think you can take him in *China*?"	.....
e	"He has to be somebody else."	.....
f	"What's happened? What's happening?"	.....

After you read

20 Havilland says that he arranged for Marie to be kidnapped to prevent a war. Do you think he was right to do what he did? Discuss your ideas with another student.

21 When he enters Beijing, the assassin changes his appearance. How could you change your own appearance? Think about hair, glasses, clothes, your age, and how you walk. Discuss your ideas with another student.

Chapters 10–11

Before you read

22 What do you know about Mao Zedong's life, and his tomb in Tiananmen Square? Use a library or the Internet to find out more.

While you read

23 Answer the questions below, using one of these names:

d'Anjou   David Webb   Marie Webb   Mo Panov   Alex Conklin
Matthew Richards   the assassin   Who:

a	takes a bus to Tiananmen Square?	....
b	does Marie contact for help?	....
c	did Webb talk to before he left the U.S.?	....
d	is trapped inside Chairman Mao's tomb?	....
e	is captured outside the tomb?	....
f	gives information to Conklin and Panov?	....
g	tells them about Lin Wen-zu?	....

After you read

24 Use one word to complete each sentence.

a The assassin dresses to look … a priest.

b Conklin's overseas career was ended … a bomb.

c Marie gets out of her taxi … the Empress Hotel.

d Conklin knows something ... Marie's situation.

e Webb fires ... two men in Mao Zedong's tomb

f Mo gives a toy bear to a man dressed ... a woman.

g Conklin hits Matthew Richards ... his wooden foot.

h Conklin wants to know who's in charge ... the operation.

i Catherine Staples is killed by bullets fired ... a black car.

25 Use these names and phrases to complete the sentences. Which sentence has different grammar from the others?

a bomb   Alex Conklin   a red flag   an enemy plane
d'Anjou   many bullets   the fire escape

a Marie left the apartment building by ... .

b David Webb's first wife and children were killed by ... .

c Alexander Conklin's foot was blown off by ... .

d Mao Zedong's body was covered by ... .

e The assassin's black suit was paid for by ... .

f Matthew Richards was trapped by ... .

g Catherine Staples was hit by ... .

Chapters 12–13

Before you read

26 After Catherine Staples' death, Alexander Conklin goes to see Ambassador Havilland at the house on Victoria Peak. Conklin is very angry. What do you think he says? Act out their conversation with another student.

While you read

27 Number these in the order that Bourne uses them in the Jinshan Bird Reserve.

a chain	.....	**d** flashlight	.....	**g** hunting knife	.....
b wire-cutter	.....	**e** gun	.....	**h** firecrackers	.....
c wire	.....	**f** stones	.....		

28 Decide whether these sentences are true (T) or false (F).

a Conklin thinks Ambassador Havilland is ill.   .....

b One of McAllister's staff works for the enemy.   .....

c Bourne ties the assassin to a fence.   .....

d The assassin uses water to slow down a flame.   .....

e Two of the three of the fuel trucks blow up.   .....

f The assassin kicks Bourne at the door of the plane.   .....

29 Bourne and the assassin are in a Chinese government
airplane. They can't simply fly across the Hong Kong border
and land. How can Bourne get himself and the assassin into
Hong Kong? Discuss your ideas with another student.

Chapters 14–15

Before you read

30 Which of these people do you think will die before the end of
the book? How? Discuss your ideas with another student.

David   Marie   Sheng Chouyang   McAllister   Havilland
Conklin   Panov   the assassin

While you read

31 How many of each of these weapons does Bourne use when
he attacks the house on Victoria Peak?

a	tear gas grenades	…..
b	fire bombs	…..
c	packages of plastic explosive	…..
d	MAC-10 machine guns	…..

32 Who is being referred to in these sentences, by the words
in *italics*?

a	"*I'm* a failure, like Alexander Conklin but without his drinking problem."	………………
b	"Because *he* wouldn't have allowed it."	………………
c	"It was that kind of thinking that lost *you* the country."	………………
d	"Surely the generous Americans or British will welcome *me*, sir?"	………………
e	"What do *you* do when there's a part of you that you hate?"	………………

After you read

33 "We all have a dark side, David. We wish we could deny it, but
we can't. It's there. Maybe we can't exist without it." Marie is
talking here. Do you think she is right? Can people exist
without a dark side? Discuss your ideas with another student.

Writing

34 Use a library or the Internet to find out more about the history of Hong Kong, from when the island first became a British colony in 1842 to its return to China in 1997, and also its more recent history. Write a report.

35 Watch the movie of *The Bourne Supremacy* on DVD. It is very different from the book. Think about the differences in the places where the story happens and the people in it. Why do you think the movie is so different? Which do you prefer? Write about this.

36 Imagine you are working at the British Embassy or the United States Consulate in Hong Kong toward the beginning of the story. You are asked to write a report on Sheng Chouyang. Use the information that Havilland gives to McAllister, and add some details of your own. Say how dangerous you think he is to world peace, and finish by recommending what to do about him.

37 Imagine that after she is kidnapped, Marie writes a letter to David. She hopes that one day he or the police will find it. In it she describes what happened to her, the men who took her away, why she thinks it happened, how she feels, and what she hopes will happen. Write her letter.

38 Use a library or the Internet to find out more about the Walled City of Kowloon. Find out why neither British nor Chinese law operated there; who actually ruled it; when it was destroyed, and what is there today. Write a history of the Walled City.

39 After she takes Marie away in her car, Catherine Staples has another conversation with her friend, the retired British detective Ian Ballantyne. She tells him what has happened, and they discuss the reasons for it. Write their conversation.

40 Beijing has been the capital of China for hundreds of years, and was the host city for the 2008 Olympic Games. Use a library or the Internet to find out more about Beijing's history, and the city today. Write a short guide for visitors.

41 When Bourne is trapped in the tomb in Tiananmen Square, he realizes that from the beginning it was a trap—from the information paid for on the rainy island to the clothes that the assassin wore. Later, he writes about how he was tricked. Tell the story.

42 Conklin says to Havilland, "Somebody arranged for Catherine Staples to die because of what she learned here." Who do you think arranged Catherine's death? Why was she dangerous because of what she had learned? Write your ideas.

43 After the fighting at the house on Victoria Peak, the local newspapers print the story. They have the photograph of the "dead" Jason Bourne and some of the facts. Write a newspaper report.

Answers for the activities in the book are available from the Penguin Readers website. A free Activity Worksheet is also available from the website. Activity Worksheets are part of the Penguin Teacher Support Programme, which also includes Progress Tests and Graded Reader Guidelines. For more information, please visit: www.penguinreaders.com.

WORD LIST

agent (n) someone who works for a government or police department in order to get secret information about another country or organization. An **agency** is an organization or department within a government that does a specific job, for example the Central Intelligence Agency (CIA).

assassin (n) somebody who murders, or **assassinates**, an important person or important people

bow (v) to bend the top part of your body forward as a sign of respect

briefcase (n) a case for carrying papers or documents

casino (n) a place where people try to win money by playing cards or other types of games

chairman (n) somebody who is in charge of a meeting or organization. Mao Zedong was Chairman of the Communist Party of China from 1943 to 1975.

colony (n) a country or area that is under the political control of a more powerful country

consul (n) a representative of a government who lives in another country to help and protect citizens of their own country living there; the consul works in a **consulate**

dealer (n) somebody who sells illegal drugs; somebody who gives out playing cards in a game

diplomat (n) somebody who officially represents their government in a foreign country

embassy (n) the building used by officials who represent their government in a foreign country

firecracker (n) a small tube filled with a powder that explodes loudly

flashlight (n) a small electric light that you can carry in your hand

gag (n/v) a piece of cloth put over somebody's mouth to stop them making a noise

grenade (n) a small bomb that can be thrown by hand

holy (adj) connected with God and religion

hosepipe (n) a rubber or plastic tube that is used to move liquid